PINK NOISE

PINK NOISE

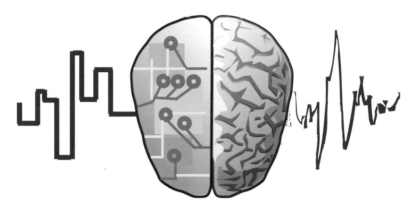

A
POSTHUMAN
TALE

Leonid
Korogodski

illustrated by Guddah

SILVERBERRY
PRESS

PINK NOISE
Copyright © 2010 Leonid Korogodski.
All rights reserved, including the right to reproduce this book, or portions thereof, in any form.
Published by Silverberry Press, P.O. Box 492, Sharon, MA 02067, U.S.A.
Edited by Elizabeth Bell Carroll. Illustrated by Guddah.

Quotes:
- page 11:   G.U. Pope, W.H. Drew, John Lazarus, and F.W. Ellis, translators. *Tirukkural: English Translation and Commentary.* W.H. Allen & Co., 1886.
- page 74:   M.D. Raghavan, translator. *A Ballad of Kerala.* The Indian Antiquary, 1932.
- page 116:   Ramprasad Sen. *A Hymn to Kali.* Translated by Sanjukta Gupta, in *Encountering Kali: In the Margins, at the Center, in the West,* edited by Rachel Fell McDermott and Jeffrey J. Kripal, University of California Press, 2003. Copyright © 2003 Regents of the University of California.
- page 141:   Daniel C. Dennett. *Consciousness Explained.* Back Bay Books, 1991. Copyright © 1991 Daniel C. Dennett.

Images:
- Front Flyleaf: *Swiss Cheese Terrain, the South Polar Region, Mars.* NASA/JPL/University of Arizona.
- page 6:   *Albedo Map of the South Polar Region of Mars.* NASA/Mars Global Surveyor.
- page 151, Top: *Galaxy M81.* NASA/JPL–Caltech/S. Willner, Harvard–Smithsonian Center for Astrophysics.
- page 151, Below: *Galaxy Simulation.* Anthony L. Peratt, Los Alamos National Laboratory. Copyright © 1986 Institute of Electrical and Electronics Engineers.
- page 153:   *Galaxies NGC 1409 and 1410.* NASA/William C. Keel, University of Alabama.
- page 158:   Derived from Gregory J. Leonard, Kenneth L. Tanaka. *Geologic Map of the Hellas Region of Mars.* Map I-2694, U.S. Geological Survey, U.S. Department of the Interior, 2001.
- End Flyleaf: *Layered Terrain, West Arabia Terra Crater.* NASA/JPL/Malin Space Science Systems.
- Dust Jacket, Back: *Geysers on Mars.* NASA/JPL/University of Arizona.

Publisher's Cataloging-in-Publication Data
(Provided by Quality Books, Inc.)

Korogodski, Leonid.
   Pink noise : a posthuman tale / by Leonid Korogodski ; illustrated by Guddah. — 1st ed.
   p.   cm.
   Includes bibliographical references.
   LCCN 2009914228
   ISBN 978-0-9843608-2-6 (hardcover)
   ISBN 978-0-9843608-0-2 (Adobe PDF)
   [etc.]

   1. Human evolution—Fiction. 2. Human beings—Fiction. 3. Cyborgs—Fiction. 4. Immortality—Fiction. 5. Science fiction.   I. Title.

PS3611.O744P56 2010   813'.6
                                                       QBI10–600022

First Edition: August 2010   10 9 8 7 6 5 4 3 2 1

The paper used in this publication is of archival quality and acid-free.

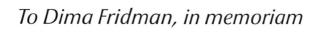

To Dima Fridman, in memoriam

The Cryptic Region, dark against
the south polar ice cap, Mars

PINK NOISE

ஐயுணர்வு எய்தியக்
கண்ணும் பயமின்றே
மெய்யுணர்வு
இல்லா தவர்க்கு
—திருக்குறள் 354

Five senses gained—

what benefits accrue

to them whose spirits lack

perception of the true?

—TIRUKKURAL, Verse 354

1

THE GIRL WAS IN A COMA SO SEVERE THAT IT PREVENTED digital upload of her mind. This rescue mission called not for a doctor but an artist. Nathi was one, the best master of brain debugging in his order.

It helped that he had no brain himself.

Almost six centuries ago, the first human mind had been successfully transferred into a digital format, becoming the world's first official posthuman. No body to age, digital backups—all this translated into a potential immortality. Some of the human race had followed suit. Their cyberspace reality, e-World, had grown in size, with hardware spread out all across the colonized part of the solar system.

But for all of that, every new transfer of a human mind was like an artist copying a masterpiece—*by hand and brush*. Despite all technological advances, analog debugging of a brain remained an art. One couldn't simply trap a thread and start examining the stack. What passed for analog threads leaked into each other, slippery, uncertain to pin down, like quantum particles in many places at the same time. Transfer from the analog into the digital, discretization of continuum, implied a loss. But Nathi didn't feel regret. His own mind had been transferred at more than 99% five centuries ago. He did not believe that the remaining less than one percent may have contained something important.

No, he must have simply lost some noise.

The girl could certainly use losing some of hers. No doctor had been able to unravel the jumbled mess the girl's mind had become. Three years ago, when the girl was ten, something had happened to the so-called *non-specific* part of the girl's thalamus—a football-shaped thing at the base of both hemispheres—causing a mass suicide of neurons. With a good-sized hole at the hub of consciousness..., well, self-awareness was out of the question.

What was he to do?

He moved inside.

Nathi sent billions of nanobots into her brain to form a local network, an extension of e-World, a temporary housing for Nathi's electronic mind. From his abode in her thalamus, he listened to the girl's brainwaves. Every specific part of thalamus was talking to the corresponding part of neocortex—visual to visual, auditory to auditory, motor ones to their counterparts for every muscle group. The dialogue between the neocortex and the thalamus continued, their neuronal ensembles oscillating in the network patterns that evolved in both space and time.

But something had to synchronize the oscillating circuits. Something had to bind the separate perceptions into a cohesive whole to create a *self* existing in a *now*—just as if one saw, heard, smelled, experienced the world in real time, even if the signals all arrived at different times into different locations in the brain, where they were processed differently and at different speeds.

That was the job of the destroyed part of her thalamus.

Without anything to synchronize the oscillations, there could be no *self*—as if she were a group of people, one of whom could only see, another one could only hear, yet another one could only move this finger or that toe, none of them communicating with the others.

Without sensory feedback from action—*any* action, even a slight shifting of eyeballs—the brain could not make sense of its environment. Even an intact brain can't perceive a true reality, always simplifying its sensory input to be able to process it within reasonable time. For this girl, the outside world simply disappeared, contracted into zero dimensions. No need for self-awareness nor consciousness, so they shut down. No movement either, other than the vegetative rote—breathe, pump blood, move bowels. Just as a fetus in a womb begins developing a three-dimensional and temporal perception by her kicks and jerks and twitches, so a completely isolated brain begins to lose, forget that same sense of a three-dimensional space and a linear time.

So Nathi did the only thing that he could think of, wiring his own electronic mind into the girl's brain to replace her destroyed *self* and to rebuild the missing integration circuit—the one ring to bind all others.

It had taken months to make it work. But finally he made her dream.

THE DARKNESS OF THE MARTIAN POLAR NIGHT IS CUT BY plumes of glow reaching for the sky. This is a distant view of the Pincushion, an array of "solar windmills" in the southern magnetic field anomaly.

Sky-tall, the power needles pierce through the Martian ionosphere, catching streamers of a violet aurora—bare glimpses in the dark, and no one to see them but this little girl, alone in an observation bubble nestled in the curve of a castle wall. But she is not afraid. She knows there is a whole world behind the seeming emptiness and silence, shimmering with invisible curtains, "too violet" for her to see. The girl imagines—prayer flags upon the lines that stretch across a floating forest; tall, thin trunks are draped with gauze of dust—the swirling skirts of dancers that will never stop.

"Prayer wheels turn round and round, make the little devils dance."

1

From all around, slender columns of electrified dust, taller than Olympus Mons, are drawn toward the even taller needles—baby dust devils, only beginning to form. They circle around the needles, spinning, like dancing partners straining for a kiss, like moths that opted for the longest path to flame. But they keep coming, one after another, to turn the flywheels stacked along the axis of the needle like toy rings around a pole. Round and round the wheels go, hovering above each other, resting on their magnetic pillows.

If only she could reach and touch them, turn the prayer wheels, maybe the Needle Fairy would grant her wish. But she is just a little girl; and outside, the world is so cold the air itself has turned to ice. Nanny is strong, and fast, in that special battle-dress of hers, and she can shoot invisible sharp fire from her fingers—so sharp it cuts through shining armor—the girl saw that, yes she did!

But Nanny flew toward the needle long ago. And she has not come back.

The girl has lost all track of time, forgot her own name. But she remembers...

...blueberries. The Martian kind, the blue-gray spherules that had always fit into her palm. The special kind, with tiny fragile stems—the hardened souls of unborn dust devils. They can sometimes be found by the base of power needles, and they carry luck—that's why all princesses in Martian fairy tales are always given some enchanted blueberries, or else the tales would not end well.

She used to have them, but she'd broken the stems.

Nanny had promised to bring her some. What if she's looking for them still?

An image flashes by—a piece of broken memory? A blueberry-rock garden, serene beneath a softly glowing sky—the setting sun is lingering upon the blanket of suspended dust. The larger boulders, each taller than herself, set up a game of shifting, diffuse shadows.

Could it be she had just such a garden back at home?

LEONID KOROGODSKI

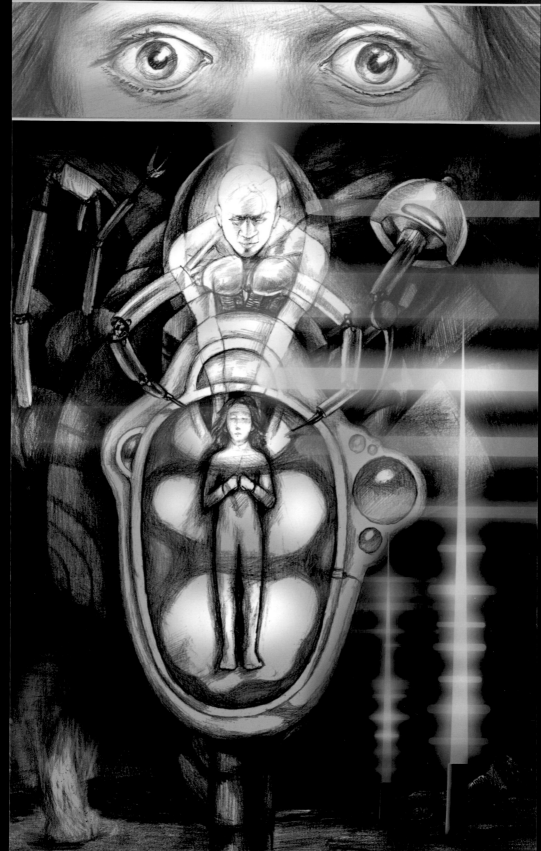

Silence. Only baby devils leaving their tracks across a layered terrain.

Wrists—writhing slowly, contorting through unknown mudras. Quick, jerky thrashing of her feet—steps of a dance that never ends, a dance that she does not control. Some strange, inhuman force invades her limbs. She always liked to dance—but not to this un-rhythm, and not to this un-music. When did this painful dance begin?

1

"Prayer wheels turn round and round, make the little devils stop."

No such luck. The Fairy keeps calling. It's now her turn to go to the needle, spin the wheels. What if her Nanny needs her help? Imagine this—her strong, fast Nanny rescued by a little girl!

A rare, nearly forgotten urge begins to build across her face, a tension pulling on her lips. She doesn't try suppressing it; she knows trying always makes things worse. She puts it out of her mind—or tries to, but she is afraid.

She *would* have laughed, but for the fear she would never stop.

NOT IF *I* CAN HELP IT.

Nathi spread himself across the myriads of nanotori-driven modulators strategically placed inside his patient's brain. If those calcium spikes got out of hand, he could selectively gate ion channels open or closed in microseconds by direct electromagnetic action—faster than by slow chemical neurotransmitters. Ion channels were the porous proteins embedded in a cell's membrane that only let the ions of particular types through, depending on the channel. If the brain were like an orchestra, then such dynamic change of the electric properties of neurons would have been like switching instruments in the musicians' hands right in the middle of a performance.

Nathi's metaphoric fingers rested on the keys of the potassium ion channels. Their activation at a few selected places

LEONID KOROGODSKI

in the neocortex would silence the neurons, putting them into the "down" state and the entire brain to sleep in waves spreading in circles at several millimeters a millisecond—the next closest thing to a break inside a digital debugger, for a brain would never stop. But that would end this dream session—only the third one in three months.

This session was especially successful. So far, she only showed some mild choreoathetosis, a syndrome of involuntary writhing, jerky movements. That may have indicated damage to her basal ganglia, an organ at the very center of her brain—the repository of her faps, fixed action patterns. Walking, running, breaking a fall or pulling a hand away from fire, driving, making love or making music—things that we can do or learn to do without getting consciousness involved. Now some echoes of her motor faps were leaking through without being called for, like fragments of a song circling unbidden in one's mind. No matter. He would fix that later. First, he had to stabilize her consciousness, recover memories....

He was at home in a human brain—this small, enclosed world of living, fragile circuits. Nathi's electronic mind washed over it like a cleansing fluid, slipped through synapses on the magnetic wings of nanobots, the microscopic nodes of his private network. With his nanotori, he could switch the brain's internal circuitry at will—but carefully, with the lightest touch, and always following the music.

Some described it as a symphony. But Nathi heard in it *ingoma ebusuku,* "song of the night," the old tiptoe music of his Zulu ancestors—perhaps because it called for no instruments, just voice. He was tiptoeing across the brain, leading a procession up and down an undulating path, out of the land of sorrows. Switch. He is with an *isicathamiya* band, singing on stage in an all-night musical contest: *Sigadla ngengoma!—We are attacking with song.* Switch. Now a *kwaito* singer of the post-apartheid era, dancing to a soul-catching electronic beat. And, hundreds of years later, in a transport spaceship, waiting with the Zulu Zionist white-robes for their historic touchdown in the Hellas basin. Swaying bodies, pointing arms. Deep voices, resonant. Polyphony developing like the converging horns of buffalo.

The drums and handclaps of a *qhuqhumbela.*

Something has changed.

A coherent wave in the theta range has snuck into the texture of the melody to couple with the faster gamma oscillations. Calcium spikes that have been threatening to overwhelm the girl's unsteady motor system have organized themselves into a pattern, binding the girl's senses to its will. The dysrhythmia's "edge effect?" But it could also be a long-term memory from the hippocampus entering the dream. So Nathi doesn't stop it. Staying in the dream the girl does not control, he watches with her eyes, and listens with her ears, smells it, feels it with her skin.

A SUDDEN FLASH OF LIGHT AROUND HER OBSERVATION bubble—a signal washing past, within the castle walls, in nanoseconds activating the alarms. They're under attack. The enemy has broken into the castle or has been secretly let in.

And suddenly, her Nanny is behind her. And suddenly, she's lifted in her arms. A second-long, eternity-worth hug—and she is passed along, into a soldier's arms. They plunge into the transport tubes—a snake of ferrofluid armor, flying at a breakneck speed, turning at the junctures, hugging the tight curves. And she is passed from arms to arms inside the flying column, surfing forward—faster, faster!

She has forgotten how to breathe. She doesn't need to yet. Between two breaths, she's coming out at the other end into a spaceport vault, and—

Flash!

Their escape shuttle explodes in its docking sheath. A gust of air, pulling—but the breach seals shut. Magnetorheological material streams out, freezing solid in the castle's emergency magnetic field. A breath of air brings a sweetish taste into her

LEONID KOROGODSKI

mouth. A voice inside her head: *You're underwater!* An osmosis mask forms out of her collar, covering her face. She didn't know she was capable of that. Wow, just imagine, and....

She doesn't know yet that tiny nanobots are busy cleansing blood of paralytic gas.

Too late. Above them, knights in shining armor are already flying out of the upper passages, in an attack formation—like a cobra poised with hood spread out. It strikes. Defenders rise to meet them in the air, the ferrofluid dark against the multi-speckled shine of diamond nanorods—their flexible emergency protection suits matched up against full battle armor.

Plasma jets crisscross the vault—the enemies have brought some heavy plasma guns, yet the defensive weaponry in the walls is conspicuously silent. One man in dark explodes in a fireball. The shock wave slams the girl against a wall. She hunkers down, sucking on her broken tooth.

A flock of crows in a thunderstorm above her head—dark crows armed with Dragonclaws. Her Nanny in the air, every finger wearing a waveguide tube of weapon-grade laser—a deadly harness over each hand. She dances in her flight with all her body, with her hands, her mudras drawing curtains of invisible sharp light. The girl can't see them, but she knows they are there—oh how do they cut through shining armor! Oh how flexible her Nanny's fingers are! She's not afraid to turn them on herself in her complex maneuvers, adjusting their power gain in milliseconds.

She is good. No one can match her, either side. She cuts the space around her in intersecting foliations, anticipating the reflection angles off the nanodiamond armor—a dance in three dimensions on magnetic wings. She flips and rolls in complicated curves—topologist of death, computing Hamiltonian potentials of evasion. She is good.

Not good enough.

A stream of plasma gushes out of the transport tube they came through, spewing bodies out—their rearguard, still flying through the tube. More enemies come out after them,

LEONID KOROGODSKI

overwhelming the girl's bodyguards with high precision fire—before the plasma trail they're flying through has even had a chance to cool. The warrior elite, they're almost a match for Nanny. Not a single hair has been singed on the girl's head.

A bubble of life surrounds her, invisible, where neither friend nor foe dares aim a weapon. The enemy is closing, unstoppable. It's obvious they want the girl alive.

And now, she is really afraid.

It is the other side of fairy tales—the horror stories of what evil wizards do to their captives, the experiments performed on their minds. She'd be a feeling, suffering "undead," her mind in pieces, literally—if she was lucky.

If she had her blueberries.

With a terrifying elegance, her mental link is snapped; she hears other voices in her head—brain hackers. She is totally cut off. The color black is leaching from the air, precipitating on the floor—in broken, mangled bodies, each covered with diamond dust.

It's so hard to reach for someone in this whirlwind.

Nanny turns. Their eyes meet in a stroboscopic contact. A moment's hesitation. Then, one killer glove moves gently, like to brush her hair.

THE GIRL'S CONSCIOUSNESS COLLAPSED JUST LIKE A HOUSE of cards, the shared tune breaking into chaos. Nathi felt the rupture like a spear stabbing in the gut, opening the body wide to let the ghost out—him. He was that ghost, for one hundred seconds of a conscious life.

He left the girl's brain, streamed back to the safety of medical peripherals, and watched through monitors, for several minutes, the girl's face. Serene, unmoved. The dead ain't easily impressed. Except, she wasn't dead.

Arms folded over her chest, her hands clenched into fists and pressed together. Legs extended and turned inward. Classical decorticate rigidity—a "mummy baby." Silent baby. The girl's eyelids didn't so much as twitch. Deep coma state,

1

the Glasgow Scale of 5. Even her reflexes were depressed. It was as if her central nervous system had refused to heed the outside world, trying to construct some other inner space, perhaps not even three-dimensional.

Just now, Nathi noticed that someone must have made her hair into curls—not long, not short, but just the right length to lie neatly by her shoulders. The burning red contrasted sharply with the clinical white of the sheets—a captured, still flame pinned down by the watchful eyes of medical equipment turning around her bed in a cylinder of vigilance.

"At least she feels no pain," her previous doctor had told Nathi months ago. "There is no 'she' to speak of. Nobody's home."

Yet. That doctor hadn't plugged *himself* into her thalamus, to fill the missing spot. Nathi knew better.

Even in a sensory deprivation tank, the brain kept generating sensory and motor context of its own—dreaming awake. The brain was like a virtual reality machine, a generator of possible worlds. Having evolved as a prediction engine, the brain churned them nonstop—in dreams or daydreams, in hallucinations or when planning for the future. Worlds of possibility.

The girl still had brainwave activity within the gamma range. Inside her brain, behind those unmoving eyelids, self-generated input for the senses—fragments of memories, sparks of emotions, failing attempts at new worldbuilding—percolated still, with nothing to connect the dots. What worlds of possibility still echoed across her mind? All Nathi did was weave the patterns once again into a single tapestry, returning her into the world she still remembered. Her eyeballs moved and eyelids fluttered—for just one hundred seconds.

Could it be that some part of the girl's "self" had survived within her digital layer? Nathi's nanobots were not alone in her brain. The girl was *parahuman,* a half-analog half-digital being that simultaneously existed in both worlds, the physical one and the cyberspace. Linked directly, parahumans interfaced with e-World at the subconscious level, just like posthumans did. But, just like humans, they had bodies. They were mortal.

LEONID KOROGODSKI

Nathi was a fairly good hacker. But he'd failed to even talk to the girl's digital half, never mind breaking in. He'd never heard of a parahuman *self* surviving only in the digital layer, but he knew that something had been going on there. *Something* that had generated the background for that dream.

That something must be running even now.

What was that? A sharp splash of activity in her anterior cingulate cortex, the seat of pain. If Nathi had a body still, he would have shuddered. The human doctor had been wrong. She *could* feel pain—if something brought all pieces of her consciousness together. What nightmares ran through the girl's comatose mind? By linking in, he'd only given them an outlet to recombine, the deaf at last finding the blind.

All of a sudden, it became too difficult to watch that serene face. Could that last dream be a real memory? How could it if the girl still lived? He knew what Dragonclaws in expert hands could do to nanodiamond armor, never mind to unprotected flesh. But dreams did not appear out of nowhere. REM sleep wasn't that different from waking state, except that input for a dream was redirected, the external stimuli replaced by an internal source.

He had himself fed the initial input. He'd lucked out when the girl recalled the blueberries. For someone with her level of amnesia, recalling them in fine detail meant that they must have been important. Yes, it was his touch—a subtle, subliminal suggestion—that had linked the blueberry-rock garden to her home in the girl's mind, but....

Where did her *Nanny* come from? No trace of her was present in the earlier, much less coherent dreams. Nathi ran again through the background data. Nothing to explain a Captain of the Dragon Guard as the girl's personal attendant.

The Dragon Guard? *Wait.* Nathi linked into his order's library. *Of course.* The Dragon Guard, the Order of Flamethrowers' famed warrior elite. Parahuman. Trained in their so-called "families" from early childhood. Their High Captain led a special, secretive commando force in the Wyrm Fleet.

1

That was some food for thought. A damn big heapful.

Following the Singularity, the old-style polities like monarchy, democracy, plutocracy—the rule of kings, of people, of the rich—had given way to caste technocracy. With one's immortality increasingly depending on technology and scientific knowledge, it came as no surprise. A parahuman's caste determined the nature of one's mind enhancements—wizards, warriors, and workers of all kinds, with normal humans bringing up the rear.

In the previous two Wizard Wars, as in the current one, the Order of Flamethrowers had always been the enemy of Nathi's order. Where could the girl have seen a Dragon Captain in such astonishingly true detail?

It was only when he started digging into data on the Dragon Guard that he discovered a curious coincidence. The girl was now being treated in the Crown of the South, a strategically important castle in the south polar region. For a long time, it belonged to the Flamethrowers—until three years ago, when they had been driven off from Mars.

Three years ago—when the girl had suffered brain damage.

But the castle had another name back then.

The *Dragon Nest.*

LEONID KOROGODSKI

2

H E DREAMED OF HELLAS, AS THE POSTHUMANS DREAM—THE
input redirected to stream out from the depths of their
digital subconscious.

Nathi dreamed of Hellas where he was born, a second generation Zulu Martian. His parents, devout Zulu Zionists, had named him Nkosinathi, "Lord is with us." But somewhere in Nathi's many wanderings, he must have lost the godly part.

Hellas was the deepest and by far the widest hole on Mars, the only place where the atmospheric pressure was enough for water to stay liquid, just above the water's triple point. The *amaZiyoni,* the Zionist Christians from South Africa, were big on baptism by immersion—*outdoors.*

He had good reasons to be proud of his people. Although Americans had been the first to step on Mars, they'd settled for a quick walk—in and out. It was Zulu, Xhosa, other South Africans that were the first to come to Mars to live.

Having failed to find the much-anticipated water in the Dao and Harmakhis Valles, they trekked westward, deeper into Hellas, until they reached the honeycomb terrain, a mess of oval and hexagonal depressions. It was only by careful, painstaking shepherding of water ice clouds forming just below the Hellas rim, and by selective damming of wind currents with osmotic nets, that finally the pilgrims learned to fill the honeycomb with water in late spring, the warmest season in the southern hemisphere.

He well remembered the day he was baptized, already a teenager—it had taken quite a while to set the cloud pastures up. Imagine wading quietly into the water, until it closes over your head. The awe mixed with a touch of fear, as you lift the helmet off to let the Martian water in—like coming out of your second skin. The air whistling out under pressure—and the sweetness of the oxygen that flows through your breathing mask. The kiss of water on your bare skin, immediately sublimating from your body's heat at this low pressure—a new birth out of a cold embrace, invigorating, sweetly painful. The thin layer of cold steam enveloping you like placenta. And the red sand swirling by your feet.

It was too long since he'd been home.

He flew—imagined wings and soared above the angular knobs of Alpheus Colles, the low mountain range known as the Nose Bridge, the images as sharp as if streamed into him by virtualization satellites in real time. A flight along the curved arc of Coronae Scopulus—a series of scarps connecting the two pockets of the honeycomb terrain, like eyes with a pince-nez over a crooked nose—and he's soaring above a honeycomb of curvilinear depressions, some already quickening with tiny hearts of fog, the silver honey. The ridges of the honeycomb rise all around him, as Nathi lands into a heavy, "tired" fog whose water's like a ripened fruit about to fall.

Around him, his *abakhaya,* "home people." Men and women, boys and girls, in sacred white, with staves, stand in the fog—it must be Sunday morning. And they sing.

A girl. A face. So familiar—who is she? She walks toward him, hangs a necklace over his neck. She points at him. She gestures with her hands. She wants him to dance.

A song picks up. What Zulu doesn't love to sing? Under his feet are round, polished stones, concealed by fog. He dances, lightly touching them. He writes his name by steps.

LEONID KOROGODSKI

The girl! He's recognized her face—his wife. But she had died in the first Wizard War, before he had become immortal. How is she here? He does not recall her name.

Why cannot I recall her name?

And where's the song? It's gone. He can't recall it anymore. The others are impatient, asking, "Has the bride danced?" No marriage is in force, until the bride has danced.

"Has the bride danced?"

But she is only walking round him, just staring with those sad, sad eyes. And now he is stamping hard, until the stones begin to crack. The guests all disappear. Children stay. They gather round him, they join hands in a grim and silent circle—then, a little girl pulls on his sleeve. The sound passing between their smart suits, through the fabric, as a tactile undertone to her words. "Please, please, the bride must dance!"

The bride must dance.

He looks back at the girl. Her face.... Serene, except her eyes—the eyes that've never opened while she has been in coma, except when his manipulators lifted up her eyelids, to reveal a blank, unseeing look. Now they're pleading.

Nathi blinks, and she is gone. They all are gone. The fog is no more. He stares at the ground—at the polished, gleaming white of human bone. At his name written all across the neat rows of skulls.

He screams. The plasma gun in his hands roars. No, not in his hands; he doesn't have them anymore. And he is not on Mars, although the sky is burning red. The air is too thick, except he doesn't breathe it, for he doesn't need to breathe. He is a posthuman, newly made and *ghosting* inside the electronic mind of an airborne InsectiEye destroyer, loaded with deadly armaments. He's confident, content. He knows none escape his roaming, all-seeing eyes. They peek among the leaves, they find each bug. They can't get out of his mental focus. None escapes.

A tiny bug lifts something, tries to aim its sting. Nathi reacts. His plasma focus gun discharges in a triple fountain—a fern-like

2

shape, with plasma leaf umbrellas on a central stalk. The blast develops in a curve to maximize area damage, burn the bugs.

But.... Suddenly, he sees. The bugs are *people*. And the sting—a little boy's Y-shaped sling with a stone. Trees are burning. The rainforest is on fire. He's on Earth. And no matter how much he cries, inside the dream he cannot shake it off—not even a bloodthirsty urge, nor blind indifference, but a serene, profound satisfaction.

2

NATHI RAN.

From visions in his dream—the burning forests, lava flows of skulls erupting from a neat arrangement of golf holes peppering mass graves the size of craters. Ran from screams, and from a silent death—the screams robbed from the dead, erupting now from his cyber-throat with a taste of vomit. Ran from a burning touch—of fire washing around his destroyer's electromagnetic shielding, and of lasers slicing through his battle cruiser's skin. The human senses running after him, invading every corner of his cyber-interfaces—images of algorithms, the bile of information streams, the tactile feel of a machine.

A taste of death. The bitterness of resurrection.

Whirling dervishes with Dragonclaws, attacking him. A vast, cold space, with tiny dots of battle cruisers thousands of miles apart—anticipation stretching taut, trajectories adjusted every microsecond, as their minds attempt to second-guess the enemy from data aging at the speed of light. The superfast space action, once within the range.

The knowledge that you can't escape this endless circle of transmigrations, that you'll be sent to yet another battle if you die. For the immortal, death was no escape.

He tried. He killed himself so many times he was afraid that he'd forget the pain, the memory of it congealing into one amorphous blob, scrubbed featureless, washed out, covered. He killed himself so many times that finally he was afraid to die, because he knew he'd rise again, reloaded, to face the

LEONID KOROGODSKI

shades in white—ancestor spirits, looking at him silently with their sad, sad eyes.

He ran, across the dream landscape of the diviners, *izangoma*. Ran from the prophetic dreams of *amaZiyoni*. But he could not escape. It was forever near, the cold presence of an Other, somewhere inside him, watching his mind—fragments of his consciousness, his memories, his torment—with its silent and inhuman eyes.

Just like he'd watched the girl's.

That thought stopped Nathi cold. He was awake, curled thin around the girl's comatose brain. His refuge. He had never thought that this was where he'd escape from pain. But—*yes, of course!* He was a physician, not a soldier. He *healed* people.

An immense relief lifted his spirit. It was only a nightmare—*a nightmare!* He had never done those things. If he had lungs, he would've exhaled, expunged the weight of pain. But, thankfully, the strange inversion of the human senses stopped. And in the glorious, profound bliss, he suddenly was conscious of the beat of the girl's brain's electrochemical circuitry.

He ran quick diagnostics, peeking into neocortex furrows, the sulci. Tiny nanotori modulators carried him across the layers of inhibitory interneurons. Nathi's mental focus burrowed through the pyramidal tract into the thalamus, examining the cortical collaterals. No change.

He lost himself in work. He held the pulse of the girl's memory formation space—the randomly connected maze of her pattern completion engine, the hippocampus. At first evolved to handle navigation, long ago it had double-teamed to handle memories and concepts. One-dimensional chains of place cells formed episodic memories, like going along a path through physical space—or a sequence of events. While two-dimensional sheets of such intersecting, forking paths formed spatial maps of the surrounding environment—or concepts, independent of specific memories....

Why couldn't he recall his wife's name?

2

2

The girl's amnesia appeared to be remarkably selective. The last dream was the first time that she had ever shown him a glimpse of home. His superiors would've wanted all that information, Nathi realized. The girl may be a daughter of someone important in the Dragon Guard.

He wondered why no one had told him that before. Why would his order keep it secret from him? He was angry. Even so, he'd been working on her memories of family and home all along, without any prompting from above—and *would* keep working. After all, they both had one thing in common—the vast, gaping holes in their memories.

However hard he tried, Nathi could not recall if he had visited his former home in the last five centuries, but surely he must have. Odd that he'd forget that. If his parents had not become posthuman later, he would've had to bury them, at least. How could he not? And if they had turned posthuman, how could he possibly not know that?

Old memories returned. Of his half-sisters on an outing for Martian blueberries, so lithe and supple, hopping up and down in the low Martian gravity—then, once back home, gobbling Terran blueberries from their inside gardens. Of his father, from the time Xolani was a junior apostle in their Church. Somehow, Nathi couldn't think of him without "junior" attached.

His mother, Sindi, leading their weekly miracle service. How she always looked incredible in the healer's sunrise-blue, wading through the sky-peach of supplicants, a rolling wave of bodies bowing and rising, crying in her wake. A multitude of voices clamoring and winding to a fervent pitch. But it is she who sets the rhythm. She's leading and not following the crowd. A touch, a glance, a word—not simply caring, but also carrying an undertone of steel. Belt sashes of pristine white lashing outward above the people sinking down to their knees, reaching the ones too far away for her to touch. And further yet—with a penetrating glance that jumps the psyche like a bullwhip's crack. People starting as if touched by the divine, shouting or bursting into tears, rolling on the ground. And

LEONID KOROGODSKI

the sashes flicking to and fro—thin streaks of white. It was by watching her that Nathi learned a healer must possess a sharper edge.

2

Sindiswa used to be an *isangoma* prior to conversion, a traditional diviner-healer. It was a mark of evil times that such as she could be accused of witchcraft, for the *izangoma* were witch-finders, enemies of the *abathakathi,* evil sorcerers and witches. But there was a short distance indeed between a healer and a poisoner. The old belief that behind every serious illness or untimely death there is an *umthakathi,* a witch responsible for bringing it, was always running strong—for superstition feeds on people's misfortune, the kind that they cannot control.

The gap between the rich and poor grew, including the affordability of posthuman immortality. With life and death increasingly dependent on technology, the technocratic cliques—the prototypes of wizard orders—increased their influence. The dwindling human population of the richest nations lived in a quite different, increasingly encapsulated world. It was a measure of their isolation that it fell to the *amaZiyoni* to colonize Mars, though the technology had been around for three centuries by then.

The old market economy stagnated. Economic crises crippled the developing world's so-called development. As wealth production all across the world came down, standards of living plunged even below the level of a preindustrial society. Mortality skyrocketed.

When it became too much to take, witch-hunts began. So many perished—burned, impaled. But although the *amaZiyoni* believed in witchcraft, they did not believe that "once a witch, always a witch." They took the accused witches in, provided they converted.

Izangoma were another matter, for they were considered to be possessed. Some thought that her *indiki* spirit would destroy her if Sindiswa entered baptismal waters. But she lived. Her spirit had apparently agreed to be baptized with her. She entered the waters twice.

34

And that was how Nathi's mother met Xolani and became his left hand side wife, days before their exodus from Earth to build a new Zion on Mars. If anything, they built a strong and happy family. Women outnumbered men two to one in most of the *amaZiyoni* communities, and rivalry between co-wives was an everyday reality. But not a few times Nathi saw his father's other, nominally senior, wife melt under one of Sindi's crack-whip glances, when he was already old enough to understand *that* wasn't rivalry.

2

Sindi quickly rose to the rank of prophetess, doing much the same thing that she did as *isangoma*—healing. She was born to that. Diviner's calling wasn't passed from parent to child, nor was the calling of healer, and yet every generation of his family on his mother's side had at least one member that their ancestors' shades had called upon.

The gift of healing was in Nathi's blood. But, strangely, he could not recall how he became a brain doctor. For he certainly did not begin as one.

When he was twenty, the time bomb of the old Earth exploded. Global Riots toppled most of the old-style governments. The age of parahuman caste technocracy began, with its new e-World economy. In order to suppress the riots, the new rulers of the world threw open the doors of posthuman immortality to recruits from the poor. Military service was the price. Nathi enlisted.

That was when gaps in his memory began to form.

Could he have done it to himself, erasing the angst and pain of war? Of war—perhaps. But memories of home? No. *Physician, heal thyself!* But he had lost his own brain five centuries ago, and one could not debug oneself. Right now, he had more important things to do.

He slid through the girl's synapses, assuming his place in the thalamus, and tried to weave himself into the song, to coax the girl's mind into remembering. He worked with kid gloves, stimulating the pontine reticular formation to release more acetylcholine. With the magnetic action of his nanotori modulators, Nathi guided ions of calcium into the SNARE proteins' ionic traps and made them bind to astrocytes—the glial cells shaped like a star. He had to make her dream.

It was a simple matter of input redirection. In that, the posthuman dreams were not much different from human ones, except that posthuman dreams were typically called by choice. He paused. Who redirected the input streams, creating *his* nightmare?

Panicking, he cut all but one of his e-World links, securing it—and was struck by the sudden silence. Until then, he hadn't realized how much e-World traffic he had carried. For a time, he simply listened to the girl's internal music—the melodies he helped create.

But Nathi also felt a noise of almost random oscillations everywhere, like the murmur of a stream. Not strong enough to make a neuron fire but, when added to the equally weak input, it could occasionally lift the signal over the threshold, making the brain unpredictable.

But not chaotic—this was no white noise, equally intense at any frequency. This noise was rising at the lower end, falling down for the higher frequencies, almost like $1/f$. The signature of something precious, something tenuous between order and chaos—complexity.

If this internal music of the brain was painted with the colors of the rainbow, combined they would have made not white but pink.

Pink noise.

Next time he dared to dream, he didn't leave the only place he felt at home. He slept in.

LEONID KOROGODSKI

3

"**H**EY, WHO IS HERE?"
The girl's voice astonished Nathi. In this lucid
dream, it came as if from Nathi's own mind. Realiza-
tion dawned—the "mummy" *spoke*.

"I am Nathi," cautiously, he tried his voice. It broke. "What's
your name?"

"I... do not know," the girl said.

He felt her puzzlement—they shared her brain.

"I cannot name myself," she added. "Can you, please?"

To his surprise, Nathi discovered that he could not—he
kept forgetting any name he now tried to give her. No cause
for panic. He was certain that he could untangle himself from
her once he woke up.

"You can't?" The girl was disappointed. "But I thought you
were my genie."

Genie?

The girl's personality traits, her emotional and intellectual
capacities, remained intact, for they did not reside in either
thalamus nor neocortex alone, but they manifested themselves
only through the interaction of the two. Just like an ancient
clock without its small arm could not tell time, while its longer
arm that gave it "personality" remained intact.

"Nathi, why is it so dark?"

The girl remembered *his* name, at least.

"Your eyes are closed," he replied, half-automatically.

"Can you open them? Genies can do anything."

He could.

3

They stood atop a sparkling staircase made of dry ice. In front of them, the grandiose coils of the castle's late *magnetica* architecture rose in their full uncloaked splendor—like a family of dragons curling around their nest, with the sparkling jewels of the observation bubbles held in their gaping maws. Within these curving walls streamed light itself, caught, bent to flow all around the castle, distorting the perspective, blurring contours. From the top, a many-pinnacled crown rose sharp into the darkness of the polar night.

"Wow."

Balancing on one foot, the girl tentatively scratched above her ankle with her heel—and Nathi felt that. So, her body map and three-dimensional perspective were intact. The air tingled with a myriad of tiny needles—*wait, what air?* Martian atmospheric pressure was so low that carbon dioxide would just sublimate in spring. But in this dream, it wasn't the dry ice that burned the skin. Their naked soles were intact. The body didn't want for air. Another sense was added to the normal five. Like a blind person puzzling out shapes by whole-body touch, he felt, so close to the castle walls, the shape of the magnetic field—wave after wave across her... his... no, *their* bare skin.

It made him want to dance.

Abruptly, sinuous convulsions started up the girl's arms and, against her will, her hands contorted through a series of strange positions, oddly graceful. The girl's legs began a slow involuntary dance.

Time to wake up. He sent the usual trigger to his nanobots—no response. Their mental presence dwindled, flickering, like ghostly pain reminding of a freshly amputated limb. Nathi felt naked. In this lucid dream, his mind was shackled

LEONID KOROGODSKI

in the narrow confines of the girl's body—a sensation he had nearly forgotten. He'd forgotten so much....

Just *how* much—and *when?* Was not his memory affected by the girl's amnesia, right now? When exactly had the gaps begun to form? Perhaps, not long ago. Maybe, from the time that he had started on the girl. He had no way of knowing.

And suddenly, he was afraid. He had to break the contact—*now!* Struggling, clawing his way out of her mind, he pushed his mental focus out, with all the force of centuries of practice—a posthuman soul desperate to leave a body. The girl's fractured defenses wouldn't hold. Just one last effort, and he would be free, but—

"Genie, can you help me dance? Please?"

Nathi turned. From outside, she looked so tiny, swimming in the ebb and flow of the plasma wind. A tingling, faint at the periphery of his awareness, his tactile senses clinging still to the girl's skin. He had an odd sensation of being stretched out.

Now! Just one final effort, and—

He would return—to what? The empty skulls of his nightmares? Or the memory-gapped loneliness? He had no home. No family. And no friends.

Her face. Serene and listless to the sharp eyes of the monitors, in the dreamworld it shone with a mix of curiosity and hope, pain and fear, and surprise. But not despair. *That* was a learned taste.

The image flickered, overlapping with the monitors' perspective—deadpan face, closed eyes, hands clenched. But in this dream, the girl was looking back at him—the only link that held her consciousness together. Did she know that? How did it look? A tunnel leading to the light? He couldn't tell; he was already half-awake. Another moment, and she'd go back to just being a human vegetable—watered and fed, with hair neatly trimmed. She'd never dance again.

The bride must dance.

He stopped.

3

The waves of the magnetic field, felt by her skin, by Nathi, formed a pattern—and he recognized it.

"Hey!" He once again forgot her name—*yes!* The amnesia had returned, which meant that he was back; the contact hadn't ruptured. *Yes!* He'd never been so happy at forgetting things. "Hey, have you ever sailed a magsail ship?"

Oh yes, she had.

He conjured magnetic sails—superconducting hoops arrayed in linked loops or spread into shifting grids. Two-masted brigantine. He was a genie, after all. "Imagine you're a ship."

The girl was at the heart of this revolving, beautiful contraption. Her eyes were filled with light. "Look!"

Their perspective changed. The castle suddenly collapsed into a tiny flower below them. They shot straight up and hovered, surrounded by invisible walls of what would have been the navigation bridge.

He settled back into her senses. "These"—he pushed the girl's awareness into her arms and legs, caught in involuntary dance—"your sail controls, at autopilot. They must dance to keep us flying. See? It's good that they keep moving."

Nathi loaded the magsail navigation model into their shared mind. Unlike solar sails, magnetic sails did not, in most cases, travel in the same direction as the solar wind. They weren't pushed but slid sideways, deflecting the charged particles into another magsail on the same mast—or even on another mast, such as a *peacock tail*. Magnetic sails allowed for unprecedented maneuverability, way ahead of any other method of propulsion. Ships with magsails really could dance in place.

Except, maneuvering a ship with more than one magsail required high skill and an unusual intuition, following the right-hand rule. The flat palm as a "surface" of the sail, with its magnetic field into the palm. The fingers pointing straight, in the direction of the solar wind. The thumb, extended to the side—the thrust.

"I know that," the girl said.

He did not expect the girl's involuntary writhing movements to actually match their flight. They did. Whatever training she'd received in her Flamethrower family, an electromagnetic intuition was ingrained in her dance movements.

But of course! She was a parahuman, wasn't she? *The Dragon Guard.* She must have had an augmented set of faps, fixed action patterns, straight from birth. So what he thought was choreoathetosis was really a preinstalled magsailing fap? He clicked their shared tongue.

3

Her feet moved—and the "ship" responded. The magsails behind them turned into a concave honeycomb. Deflected, the charged particles imparted a momentum—

"Hey!" The sky turned upside down. Nathi swung their left arm, turning the falcon mast like the long arm across the surface of a clock, to compensate. "Hey, careful around the peacock tail."

"These arms are *mine!*" She lightly slapped her forearm, laughing. "Falcon topgallant—quarter-turn, the mast in staggered half-spiral!" The fingers of her other hand turned—and the falcon mast's sails twisted into helix, relative to the topgallant sail.

That saved them from careening right into the shining surface of the polar ice cap. "Genie, you can have the legs. Hey, peacock tail—unfold!"

She laughed. *She laughed!* Incredible, but she regained control over her limbs. The strange dance still continued, but—the girl directed it. She danced. *They* danced.

And she was not half-bad.

"Right on, ma'am!"

They soared above the whiteness of the polar cap, swimming in the river of charged particles, feeling their magnetic touch on their skin.

"Laceland ahoy!"

The edges of the polar cap already had been speckled with the lacework of swiss-cheese terrain. The cheese was mined by little spacemen mice—

3

How odd that he should think that! The idea must have floated up from somewhere deep within the dreaming girl's subconscious. But, right now, Nathi felt as if it were his own.

Aye for the world of dreams! He thought that he could almost see the spacemen mice throw their little hard hats up in cheers—no, these were geysers of abiogenic oil, breaking out from beneath the ice and sublimating in thin air.

They skimmed over the almost geometrical patterns of "dalmatian spots," marked by the interacting streamers of the solar wind. Here, the lines of the interplanetary magnetic field passed almost vertically though the surface, having skirted over the local magnetic field anomaly.

The girl laughed, spun. What Zulu wouldn't break into a song at times like these? The song was pulsing, bursting from his mind. He didn't care what the words. It was the very act of singing, his being able to sing, that gave the song its meaning, that confirmed his self—a geno-song. He felt alive.

They danced up in the air on magnetic wings. The famous layered terrain of the Cryptic Region spreading out far below—terrace upon terrace, a filigree of color bands. They flew above the wrinkled land of Australe Sulci—so dense it looked as if the planet's brain had been left bare by the sharp edge of Australe Chasma, cleft into hard rock. They skimmed it, veering northeast.

The Needle loomed before them.

"Needle ahoy...."

The words trailed out into silence. They had stopped. Sky-tall, the Needle looked as if it pierced through the heaven's firmament itself; its top was lost to space. Encased in spinning flywheels—rungs of an impossibly tall ladder up—the Needle thrummed with energy. It pulsed through their skin. It gripped like deep vibrations of a *kwaito* beat. It pulled. It made him want to *touch*.

Must go.

The urge was pounding inside his mind.

Must reach.

44   LEONID KOROGODSKI

Must find the Fairy.

Must touch.

"Please?" the girl asked. "Let's go, hurry! We must turn the wheels. She's waiting."

"Who?"

"The Fairy. You haven't heard?"

"No." Nathi was too old for fairy tales.

"Then listen. Once upon a time..."

3

• • • THERE WAS A FAIRY. BUT SHE WAS STRANGE, UNLIKE the other fairies. She didn't swim inside the Sun. She didn't ride on comet tails. She didn't even grow Martian blueberries in her cupped hands.

"What good is she?" said everyone.

They asked her questions, told her what they wished to see her do—this thing or that one, going from up to down on the entertainment value scale. But she ignored them.

For the fairy was deaf.

"What powers does she command?" they wondered.

They waited for her word—of power or wisdom, even for a squeak to laugh at. But they only wasted time.

Because the fairy was mute.

"Then let us show her the things we fear, everything we crave for."

But they tried in vain to move her or to scare her, to plead before her, to embarrass her, to push her, to caress her, or to beat her. For she didn't feel a thing.

And she was blind.

"My, what a worthless fairy!" the people said. And they decided to forget her, for a worthless fairy makes worthless memories, and memory comes at a price.

Except one little girl. "My, what a poor fairy," she said.

She didn't know what she wished for. But she had to speak, for someone had to listen *for* the fairy. She spoke from her heart—and listened.

For the fairy was deaf.

The girl was weak and small, neglected and abused. But she did not give up, for someone had to speak the words of power and wisdom. She grew up, and spoke them.

Because the fairy was mute.

The girl did not close her eyes on evil and injustice, did not become inured to others' pain—nor did she shy away from love and friendship. Someone had to live life to the fullest, sharing its joys and suffering with others. So she looked for those others, found them, and looked *with* them.

But not the fairy—she couldn't feel a thing.

And she was blind.

3

THE BRIGHT PALE EYE OF JUPITER IS HOVERING JUST OVER the dark horizon, by the Needle's base. The planets are approaching inferior conjunction.

"It is time," the girl says. "Go."

And she cuts the link.

All of a sudden, Nathi is alone—a naked spirit caught within a lucid dream. "Wait!" The girl's consciousness is gone. *How could she do that to herself? To me?*

With an incredible force, something fans out the streams of particles. Their dream contraption of imagined sails is caught in a magnetic storm. It carries Nathi at increasing speed toward the Needle. "Fold!" he tries, but he's already lost control. He's never had it to begin with. It is clear now—sharp and obvious as the enormous blades of flywheels in his face.

The girl could not have done it on her own.

Less than a blink, and he is in the gap between the wheels, the Needle's axis thrumming straight ahead of him with a colossal current. A detector eye snaps open and swallows him whole, in a blink.

Kidnapped. Somehow, they must have tricked his digital "sleepwalking" self to beam himself out of the castle in a stream of laser signals focused on a dime—a spy detector of a tiny size. Inside—a two-dimensional array of laser nanocavities, electrically pumped. Here, light itself can be confined, not physically

LEONID KOROGODSKI

as each individual photon (this is no black hole), but in stable oscillation patterns—for information storage. A "gray hole." A spy's dream, so impossibly hard to detect next to the power needle. Nathi's consciousness is spliced across a honeycomb of cells much smaller than the light's wavelength. He's packed so tight his thoughts are being torn by quantum interference. A genie in a bottle, stored away for an eternity.

He barely has time to think, *So, back to square one.* Regret. His backup may not do as good a job. *Just don't give up, girl.*

And he's off.

How does it feel—to be a ray of light? You're cutting through the plasma of the solar wind at nearly the speed of light in vacuum. The distances have shrunk. Your world's escaping from you at the speed of light in tenuous plasma. You're a pulse of signals, ones and zeroes. A frozen state of mind.

If this were total vacuum, time would have stopped. You could have traveled millions of parsecs and still find yourself caught in the same moment of time. Only, this isn't quite a vacuum. Permeating the entire solar system is the solar wind. It slows the light down—not by much, but it's enough to make the signal pattern change.

You cannot think. You *are* thoughts frozen in transit. But you will remember dreams of plasma, of the solar wind. They change you. They imprint your consciousness with memories of distant solar storms, intense magnetic fields of Jupiter's magnetosphere, and the high megaamperes of the Io–Jupiter electrical discharge.

In the arithmetic of special relativity, this close to the speed of light, even a tiny change in speed translates into relativistic difference. You're stretched in both space and time. You're smeared across the electromagnetic spectrum. The older you is Doppler-shifted into red, the younger into blue. You feel the ages of yourself as colors.

You shall never be the same.

A noise is added to your most private, innermost structures. A pink noise.

3

3

And then you are caught, received by something at the other end. A spaceship, camouflaged with a polaritonic cloak—a thin skin that catches light within itself by binding photons to the oscillation states of nano-lattices. The captured light flows all around the ship's hull like fluid, leaving at the other end as if it passed through empty space, to make the ship invisible.

You flow, too—a thin overlay of consciousness, enveloping the hull and sliding off. But you don't exit in the same direction. You are bounced sidewise, to another ship. You follow the nodes of a relay chain, allowed to think during the brief time of your polaritonic-coupled existence; you are scanned and queried in transit.

Then, your journey ends inside the self-aware, thinking skin of a magnificent magsail frigate. That's when you find it's barely begun.

4

"**H**ELLO, BEAUTIFUL."

Who? What? Nathi readjusted his perception. *Where am I?*

He was immersed in an odd space, bodiless—his mind's eye simply hanging there like a dot. The space was filled with light, somehow centered on him and fading slowly in all directions, infinitely—he could not perceive an end.

"Welcome aboard the Dragon Guard ship DareAngel. Sorry, but we cannot tell you more."

His mental focus swiveled around to face the voice. An image, vaguely like a cloud, *magnified* in front of him—now it was far away, now very close. The distance changed, although he could swear that the object didn't leave the same spot in the three-dimensional perspective.

What the hell?

He must be in a virtual perception space of more than three dimensions. But even though he could think of such things in abstract terms mathematically, he could not visualize it. Having been a human once, his mind was stuck in three dimensions—at least, without some radical software "surgery."

"My, what a gorgeous mind! Look, folks."

Dozens of other images converged on him from all directions.

"Why, yes, indeed. But so... three-dimensional."

"Hey, stop!" he shouted. The roiling clouds made him dizzy. "Who are you?"

The "clouds" stopped and stared—he couldn't find a better word. Within, he couldn't rest his eye on anything, as if some movement had been happening in the extracurricular dimensions—so fast it came across as instantaneous change, non-stop.

4

"We are the ship. The DareAngel. You are Nathi."

There was a bare hint of question at the end.

"Alright. I see." He was within the shared perception space of an annoying bunch of artificials. But what made it his perception space?

"Hey, that's not nice. We all are equal here. And we are not a bunch. We are a ship. You must be seeing our crew interface partitions, one per member. Our personettes."

"Okay. No offense." *So then, a plural artificial. Or is it artificial pluralist?* Nathi recalled that he was kidnapped by force and trickery. He didn't have to be polite. "You too are not exactly nice. First you kidnap me, call me three-dimensional...." He wondered if that was an offense. "And how come you listen to my thoughts?"

The DareAngel grumbled. "We apologize. We have to keep an eye on you while you're quarantined, so we've co-opted you as one of our own for a while. Ah..., welcome." There was a pause, as if they were embarrassed they forgot their courtesies.

One of the cloud images slid closer up to him and, Nathi could have sworn, batted her "eye"—the winks of interchanging light and shadow. "I'm Rina. I will be your welcome personette."

He almost groaned. "Tell me first what's going on. What does it"—*fucking*—"mean I'm quarantined?" Too late, he realized that, of course, they received his thoughts. *Some welcome!*

"Sie/her/hers" are the pronouns to address an artificial (aka artie), from "she" with "h" removed.

If his welcome personette was flustered, sie didn't show it. "It means that your mind must be scanned for viruses. Once this is done, only your healer wizard will have access to your mind, only on your permission. But for the time being, you're isolated from e-World until we're sure that your Wish is neutralized."

LEONID KOROGODSKI

"My—what?"

"Your Wish. All posthumans in your order, and in many others, are infected with that virus. They use it to control your actions."

And that was how Nathi learned what all three Wizard Wars were really about.

F REEDOM.
Truth could be so painful, cold and cruel.
Nathi stared into the hurricane eye of the Great Red Spot of Jupiter, the gases churning in a double spiral three times the size of Earth. His quarantine was over. But not the pain. The pain was only just beginning.

"Have you ever heard," he asked Rina, his welcome person-ette, on their private channel, "anything about *hemineglect?*"

A brief pause. "We have now. It's described in our database as a human neurological condition, when a patient can't perceive one side of space. In one type of hemineglect, it's the entire left or right half of the field of view—although it affects all senses—but objects appear whole in the other half. While in the other type, the patient can perceive only one half of every object—even one's own body—anywhere in one's field of view."

"It doesn't mean much to you, does it?" Nathi said. "Can you imagine seeing other people all one-eyed, with only one half of the eye? If one was born that way, one wouldn't know better. But hemineglect can happen to adults as a result of serious brain damage. Then, one knows how the world ought to be."

"It must be terrible," the personette said. "Like one half of the entire world is missing."

"No. This is not how it works." A stab of pain. "The worst thing is: no matter that you know how it ought to be, you do not feel that anything is missing in your world. At. All."

Rina was silent.

"Only when you're cured, do you begin to feel the loss."
And, God help me, it hurts.

4

4

He now felt as if he had unwittingly neglected the true side of what he did, perceiving just the false one. Thinking that he did one thing, while doing something different. The world was slowly revealing its dark, hidden side he never knew existed.

Hidden memories returned. Of minds manipulated by the "Fallen Watchers," as his new friends often called the enemy. Of so many posthumans made to kill—yes, even their own children—with deep satisfaction in their minds, without realizing that. Of Nathi's own art used to defeat the prisoners' mental defenses, turning them into posthuman marionettes just like himself—a fate far worse than death.

He'd thought he only healed!

He'd had but an *illusion* of free will, enslaved by the Wish virus.

Not anymore. Here, at the military station of the Order of Flamethrowers in orbit around Jupiter, Nathi regained his freedom—at the price of pain.

What had he *done?*

How Nathi had become a brain debugging artist, while most posthumans served as soldiers, was a mystery. Inborn resistance? His ancestor genes? A posthuman's mental growth usually was stunted under compulsion by the Wish. His former order maintained special crèches where they grew future posthumans. Upon reaching their "graduation" age—sufficiently developed but still malleable teenagers—crèche-grown humans had their minds transferred, bodies discarded, though not before they gave enough of their sperm and eggs to make more children for the crèches. They were even bred for certain traits.

Some of the Fallen Watchers called it "a happy childhood on a farm."

With the external e-World sensors, Nathi watched the Dragon Guard ships dance in space. He couldn't find a better word for that. With a small but ever-present, ever-changing thrust from their sails, they could ignore the orbital dynamics of free fall. In a magnetosphere this complex and powerful,

LEONID KOROGODSKI

4

they spun and flipped, maneuvering so fast that it was dizzying to watch. They were alive—intelligent shapeshifters, morphing their hulls in flight to fit the dance. Beings of grace and beauty.

Humankind had long dreamed of creating artificial intelligence, yet dreading we would only make heartless machines. Who would have thought that our mind's children would be as emotional as we are? They would have to be. No emotionless computer could compute free movement in response to unpredictable and arbitrary input. Too many degrees of freedom, too little control, too strong the butterfly effect. We had to reinvent emotions, this time as an optimization mechanism for fast decision making—although, condensing a report on thousands of flight parameters into a single human face to show to the pilot had been done for centuries. Free movement was ingrained in the human mind—no, *any* mind—the neverending loop of action–feedback–action building the internal model of the world. We knew no other. Thought itself was motion internalized.

So beautiful, he thought. *And so vulnerable.*

Not physically, but in cyberspace. Like him.

"Do you know what I'd like to morph to, if I could?" the personette said.

"No. What?"

"A ballerina." Sie sighed.

Of all things, sie desired a human body! Nathi didn't know what to say.

"I so love to dance," sie said.

The bride must dance.

He heard a bell. A human shape "materialized" in Nathi's simulated sensory environment—an avatar of his personal healer, a gentle woman with tired eyes. How many posthumans had she "cleaned" by analyzing their minds? He hoped that the healer wizard corps had their hands full with other rescued posthumans. But he knew the war was not going well for the Order of Flamethrowers of late.

"*Sawubona,* Nathi," she said. "It is time for our next session."

He'd debugged so many brains! It was his turn to have another person look into his mind and probe his shame, his innermost pain—just like he'd done back in the castle with the girl.

4

H E LIVED THROUGH AN INCESSANT STREAM OF DIGITAL nightmares. Children burning in the jungle. In baptismal pools, the sacred Martian water boiling from the heat of blood. His mother, standing over the piles of skulls in healer's blue—an apparition? e-World presence? He may never know if she had survived, or if she had become a posthuman. All that mattered was in her eyes—forgiveness.

Why?

In burning shame, he felt the presence of another deep within him, analyzing his mind into cluster units and their subclusters and their subclusters too—the intertwining, multitiered constructs of his reality, the nested fractal patterns of his consciousness—deriving first- and higher-order Rényi entropies, manipulating clustering and integration indexes. Except, this time it wasn't the inhuman presence that had watched him run through the nightmares back on Mars. For that had been the Fairy that the girl carried in her digital substratum, thus infecting him.

Wish Fairies were purely cyber-beings that had appeared mysteriously in e-World before the current war began, but they were no viruses—they didn't reproduce. Nobody knew where they came from. No faction claimed credit for developing them. No one was able to communicate with a Wish Fairy either. They were too alien, impenetrable, as if their perception space was zero-dimensional, contained all in a single point—a singularity. But they did their job unfailingly, without prompt.

They came into e-World in order to destroy the Wish.

Some thought they had been sent by aliens. Some, that e-World had developed a global consciousness, of which Wish Fairies were avatars. Some, that the Fairies were sent by God, as living spirits breathed into a lifeless world, God adding His touch to man's creation. Some, that they came from

LEONID KOROGODSKI

the devil, to seduce the posthumans to leave Eden and come back to Earth.

For Nathi, all that mattered was that his little girl carried a Fairy, and that she cared about the girl.

He had to go back to save the girl. But first, he had to be cleansed of any backdoors the wizards of his former order may have hidden in his digital mind.

4

ONCE UPON A TIME, WHEN BRAINWAVES WERE DISCOVered, researchers used to marvel at how brains worked so well despite the noise, for the exactness of a digital computer was held up as a model of perfection.

But, that very noise, those same oscillation patterns, *were* the mental states. Continuously changing, they were both the data *and* the process. Brains did not have fixed routines and algorithms—unlike the primitive instructionist computer architectures that were easy to debug, to keep under control. Back in the early days of cyberdom, developers aimed to design all chaos out.

But the instructionist computer architectures couldn't support consciousness. Nothing designed could. Brains *evolved.* As a brain grew, its neurons formed connections with each other in a process very similar to natural selection. In a grown brain, neurons competed for a chance to fire. The winning connections were rewarded with stronger synaptic strength—they were remembered, selected to embody memories of the sensations and adaptive actions, making possible their repetition, recollection, or imagining—the brain was learning. The brain's oscillation patterns were being *selected* for the best fit. For the evolutionary process worked wherever competition, memory, and variation could be found.

For it was the variation that made brains work.

The pink noise.

The brain would never give the same exact response to the same input. Its neurons spontaneously self-organized, without any master clock. Their synchronization remained transient and ever shifting. Interacting, the brain's billions of oscillators randomly adjusted their phases, now forward, now back, creating "noise"—the brain's internal context, not determined by but only modified by the external input.

White noise is just a random nonsense. But this noise was pink—a fractal noise, a product of the "neural evolution." Every previous decision influenced the ones to come in unpredictable ways—a long memory effect. An imperceptibly small change could easily result in sharp swings in response—as if the brain were in a phase transition state, like ice and water at the melting point, except one didn't know which direction it would take. The resonances were unstable, branching out into many states—just like a ball atop a hill deciding where to roll.

Brains *chose*.

In the digital world, in comparison, all resonances were predictable. Irrational clock multipliers had been meant to compensate for that. Only, the Wish subverted those multipliers to be rational. That made the posthuman minds just as deterministic or chaotic as their input was. The rest was the control of their environment. The virus made sure that the posthuman minds did *not* return from a predictable state, sinking instead into a stable balance in a "low potential pit" of undiluted rationality. It lured them by providing what they wanted—leading to the thing they wanted next, more and more predictable each time.

But easy life is easy to control. At first, it looked as if your wishes were being fulfilled. Then—you may think that you're playing just another virtual reality game, while actually you're killing real people.

That was what gave the Wish virus its name.

FOR THE FIRST FEW HEALING SESSIONS, NATHI WAS LOCKED in his private world. But later, he was often asked to manifest his avatar into the healer's physical environment. To any parahuman present at the same location, he would suddenly appear out of thin air—a visible and audible, and even smellable and touchable projection. A few times, he looked upon it from the outside, via the e-World interaction sensors installed in the healer's garden.

He discovered it felt like talking to a complex animation overlaid upon the real world—the false within the true. He didn't hide these thoughts, for they remained between him and the healer wizard. For these sessions in the garden, he was left alone even by his welcome personette, who otherwise kept fast to him.

4

But they were interrupted once.

A stand of bamboo parted in a wave, washing around someone slithering through, and a woman stepped into the clearing. Nathi was struck by more than the familiar bright red of her hair. Something in her face was shining through the wrinkles and the hardened eyes—something he had found in the girl when she had been dream-dancing in the air, the ignited heart of a magsail brigantine.

He also noticed the signs of many alterations to her motor system. The degrees of freedom in her movement were amazing. Next to her, an ordinary human would have looked like a gorilla next to a nimble dancer—in agility, but not in strength. This woman could cut steel with her bare hands.

The Dragon Guard.

How could he miss this in the girl? Another side of his "hemineglect of truth," induced by Wish.

The healer wizard bowed. "Your Highness."

Nathi stared. Non-wizard nobility was *rare*.

This must be their High Captain.

"You may rise."

Belatedly, Nathi remembered to bow too.

The woman glided over to Nathi's avatar. But in e-World, her eyes locked with his. They seemed to say, *So. It was you who shared my daughter's mind.*

The healer made to leave.

"Please stay." The noblewoman gestured. "He is your patient."

You have been into his *mind,* she must have left unspoken.

"I am Naomi," said the Dragon woman. And, immediately, to the healer: "Status. Is he clean?"

The healer wizard frowned. "Fairly. I am inclined to think that he has no backdoors left, but... I would like to run him through more diagnostics."

4

"We may not have the luxury," Naomi said, her eyes still fixed on Nathi. "The decoy that we have left to mask his absence cannot hold forever. It is getting anxious."

Left where? At the castle?

"Am I going back?" he said.

Naomi narrowed her eyes. "Afraid? You should be."

As if from far away, he saw his avatar shake his head in a no. "Yes. But it's irrelevant." *My life is nothing, all the centuries of it.* "I have to go back to save the girl."

Naomi's eyes bore into him. "We aren't like your former order; we can't *order* you to go back. We cannot *make* you go. Do you understand the risk?"

"I do." He nodded.

"You can be retaken. You already know what it means. We cannot even trust you with the plan of our attack. We'll have to erase memories—*again.*" The woman's presence was over-powering. "We cannot make you do it. Do you understand?"

If he still had a throat, it would have been parched. It was his choice.

"I do," he said.

"You may not, in the end, be able to rescue her. Your sacrifice may be for nothing, and you shall remain in mental slavery—perhaps, forever. *Do you understand?*"

He felt a quietly supporting presence of his personette—and her anxiety.

"I do," Nathi repeated for the third time. "I must try to save her." From his former owners trying to enslave her mind. "I know how."

"Yes! I knew it!" Rina sent on their private channel.

For the first time, Nathi saw Naomi smile.

LEONID KOROGODSKI

5

WHEN NATHI LOOKED BACK AT HIMSELF—THE SHELL that they had left behind, to keep the castle unaware of his absence—he did it with entirely new eyes.

To look was to arrive, for Nathi once again was turned into a pulsing ray of light, beamed back into the castle from the military base of his new friends in orbit around Jupiter. But when he stepped back into the thin shell of his external interfaces, Nathi knew he had to die. No one could blame him for the things he'd done, so he condemned himself. A voluntary exile from the Eden of immortal life.

It was the time to make himself garments of skin.

He had to save the girl.

He didn't know all the details of their plan—was not supposed to. He knew that it included an attack against the castle, but he had to get the girl out of the danger zone first.

"Hi, Genie! Has the Fairy destroyed your Wish?"

She greeted him with a happy mental dance when he reactivated her dream world on his arrival. He was pleasantly surprised. She could remember things. More than he did. He had forgotten the girl's real name—again.

"I see that you have met her," Nathi said.

They shared a smile.

כתנות
עור

"What did you ask her?" she said.

Ask? "She didn't talk to me." He simply... knew.

"She never does. The Fairy is mute, remember?"

Nathi couldn't speak, dumbstruck. *So that was no fairy tale.*

"And she is also deaf," the girl said. "But you gotta ask. Because you will get nothing if you don't."

True knowledge doesn't come without doubting first. Nathi understood. The sharpest knowledge also came with screams. "What did *you* ask?"

The girl did not reply at once. She led his mental eye into the labyrinth of transport tubes. Up, up the dark and empty dragon veins they rose, all the way back to the observation bubble. Nathi recognized the place at once. The needles reaching for the sky. Baby dust devils. And the dry ice of the polar cap, shining faintly through the blanket of the polar night.

But this time he was looking with new eyes. This time, he saw the battle laser installations sprayed over the castle walls like pearls. The patterns of "dalmatian spots" beginning to appear in the polar ice revealed the traces of retractable sheaths of nuclear missile batteries, ready to spring up from their underground bunkers, each launcher primed for bursts of long-range automatic fire. Wizard interdiction amplifiers, to disrupt the enemy communications and to blind their devices and to worm into their ships' computer brains themselves.

By the neuromorphic principle, each more advanced computing architecture further bridged the gap between process and data. The Singularity breakthrough had been achieved down that path—a kind of evolution in its own right. But high performance and the possibility of electronic consciousness came at a price. It meant some bad news for security, for execution of data had become almost synonymous with its receipt.

Warriors had special physical abilities, while wizards ruled the cyberspace. Wizard support became as critical, if not more so, as air support and space support used to be—for disrupting enemy communications, compromising their navigation data, and infecting their weapons and their decision-making systems.

LEONID KOROGODSKI

And deep down, miles below the castle, with the sharpness of a high-enhancement sensor, Nathi felt the deep hum of the generators of a mini-magnetospheric anti-plasma shield. He gaped. How... what... they wanted to storm *this?*

The girl must get away first. By the plan, they had to reach the Needle. Speaking of which.... Nathi observed how the field of ice around the castle was awash with multiple detector curtains. Suddenly, he saw the girl just as a child, so alone, so small in this cold world, her little body stretched and listless on a bed, now dreaming only thanks to him.

"I asked"—the girl was staring toward the Needle—"how to forget my mom, my family, my home. How to erase it so that it never would come back." She shut their eyes. "So that they couldn't make me hurt them."

That was how Nathi knew. Her Nanny didn't try to kill her on that day, although she could have—and indeed, was sworn to. Inside the fractions of a second they had left before it would have been too late, her Nanny made a difficult decision. She gave the girl the Fairy, transmitting with a touch of laser light—protection against mind control.

"She left toward the Needle, for support," the girl said. "And she promised she'll return. With blueberries."

I'd rather die.

It wasn't by the Dragonclaws that she was turned into a human vegetable. It was by the ministrations of his order's "doctors" who had tried all they could think of to subvert the girl's subconscious, meddling with her brain in order to emplace triggers of unconscious action, turning her into a ticking bomb against her parents when they exchanged the prisoners.

She had been only ten, three years ago, when this very castle, called the Dragon Nest by the Flamethrowers, had been taken from them by force and treachery. Three years since the Order of Flamethrowers had been expelled from Mars. Now he knew she hadn't spent them all in coma. That would've been a mercy.

She was stronger than he was.

A touch of mind on mind. "You can't be bad. You must have asked the Fairy how to become a doctor, long ago, right? You simply don't remember that."

She didn't know that he didn't have the Fairy back then.

5 FROM THAT POINT ON, THEY MET IN EVERY DREAM. NOW Nathi knew exactly what he had to do to bring her back to life. He knew that they could do it, too—could bind their minds not just in dreams, but in the waking world. But at a price—he knew the symbiotic union would not be easily dissolved. Most likely, they would have to stay together unto death.

The challenge of restoring the girl's consciousness, however, paled next to the material components of the plan. It was not just the matter of escape, but also of survival in the harsh Martian environment, and of avoiding a recapture.

Nathi's chances of convincing anyone to stash hard-duty military suits inside the room were infinitesimally low. But he never lacked in medical supplies. His work on the girl's brain was given top priority. But even so, procuring iron oxide nanoparticles in sufficient quantity proved challenging. The irony! That was the very stuff the Martian soil was made of. Nathi had to wax nostalgic, asking for a sample to be brought from his ancestral land.

He put it to good use.

This kind of nanoparticle was a workhorse of medicine from as far back as the late 20th century, the dawn of nanotech. Binding easily to proteins and DNA, they were magnetically guided to deliver their load anywhere with high precision—liver, brain, you name it. This time, it was skin.

Pretending he was harvesting new neurons from certain cells in the girl's skin, Nathi applied the powerful machinery of alternative gene splicing to coax the skin's collagen- and keratin-producing cells into altering the folding patterns of those basic building blocks of hair, skin, and nails. Binding with the iron oxide nanoparticles, these tough and fibrous

LEONID KOROGODSKI

proteins could now be rearranged in complicated beta-sheet and alpha-helix patterns at a wave of Nathi's "magic wand"—the powerful magnetic fields of nanobots.

Now he could turn the girl's skin into silk.

"Abracadabra, voila, and.... Just imagine it—the purest, softest silk."

No, he did not reorganize the instrumented molecules in groups of pleated beta-sheets with randomly coiled intervals to turn her skin into a real silk. Not really. They practiced skin control in dreams.

"What color will it be?" she asked him.

"Anything you want. Yes, even polka-dot." They smiled. "But, left unmodulated, it'll be red. You're truly Martian now, daughter of the Martian soil."

She sighed. "I'd rather be invisible."

"Well, actually, you can."

"I can? But how?"

"Hold your breath." He had already preinstalled the necessary triggers.

Abracadabra, voila, and—

"Wow!"

—light is trapped.

"Relax, and let it flow over your skin."

5

H E CALLED IT *METASILK,* FOR IT WAS A METAMATERIAL, THE kind of substance whose physical properties depend not so much on what it's made of but on how, on its internal structure.

Until then, metamaterials had mostly been made from various electrical conductors—metals such as gold and silver—or semiconductors. Nathi came up with a new design to make her skin invisible.

With the right pattern of rings and wires, and of other geometric shapes on nano scale, one could create a quantum lattice with a restricted set of stable oscillation states—*surface plasmons.* A photon striking such a surface would bind with an oscillation state, producing a *polariton*—a quasi-particle that could be guided through the lattice to another place where a photon would then be released, identical to the original one.

In this way, light could be trapped and made to flow over the surface. If it were let out at the opposite end in the same direction, an observer would look straight through such metamaterial without seeing it. It would appear that the light had never strayed from a straight line. One would be invisible—or close enough.

Varying the patterns, the same trick could be performed for other frequencies as well, from radio to ultraviolet. But no such polaritonic cloak could provide protection at all frequencies at once. Nor was it possible to be invisible from all directions at the same time. They would have to choose and constantly adjust the range of visible directions, making it as narrow as possible.

But Nathi didn't have the fancy nano-shapes of gold and silver. So instead, he folded and arranged the instrumented proteins in such a way that the *remaining* space, filled with free electrons and ions plentiful in any living tissue, formed the necessary patterns. And what's more, he could reshape patterns at will, to switch protection to another range of frequencies.

One was especially important—infrared, for it meant heat.

"WE'LL HAVE TO BE INVISIBLE IN INFRARED TO DODGE the castle security," Nathi explained. "But it'll be even more important outside."

Outside. It was her turn to reach the Needle.

She remembered. "We will be back," Nanny had sent her over the laser beam. "Hold on."

She didn't see her Nanny blast another hole in the wall. She only felt it over her skin, right through the surface of the spacesuit that her captors stuffed her in, already halfway down the transport tubes. It found her, the pressure wave, it pulled—except the enemy was stronger.

I'd rather be dead.

She didn't see her Nanny and the few remaining guards escape to reach the Needle for support. They didn't break the wall until she left the vault—the only one without a proper suit to go out.

That reminded her. She asked him, "Will we have a battle-dress like Nanny's?"

"No."

She froze. "How will we breathe?"

5

E VEN KNOWING THE PLAN, HE FELT UNEASY.
In this little body lying in a coma, trillions of living cells depended on a supply of oxygen. From the most superficial layer of her skin down to the center of her brain, her spinal cord, the marrow inside her bones, the chemical reactions of the oxygen cycle ran non-stop, transferring electrons from molecule to molecule, creating voltage gradient. Embedded in the mitochondrial membranes, the molecules of ATP synthase enzyme formed tunnels for protons to pass through in an electric current. As they passed, the protons rotated the long stalks of ATP synthase, causing them to make the molecules of ATP—the currency of life, the source of energy all cells required to live.

This was what we breathed oxygen for—to rotate the molecules of ATP synthase. This was the bottom-line of breathing.

But the electromagnetic fields of Nathi's nanobots could do that, too.

Still, Nathi felt uneasy. *Will we have enough?*

"We'll borrow some energy from the captured light," he said.

Thus risking exposure. Holding breath, if only in imagination, wasn't such a random choice of trigger. They may need to do that too to compensate for any loss of heat. Air was a poor heat conductor, and the Martian air, only one percent the density of Earth's, was even worse. On Mars, one froze mainly from the radiation loss. With their metasilk, that would be minimized. But, though much more slowly, they'd still keep losing heat.

The energy required for this to work would strain the nanobots' capacity. They'd have to reach the Needle quickly to recharge.

"Now try to pull an object with your eyes, toward yourself," he told the girl.

"Wow."

5

Nathi was impressed himself. The superlenses were made from a so-called "left-handed" metamaterial that bent light in a "wrong" direction, on the same side from the vertical. Such lenses could resolve things even smaller than the light's wavelength. They could see molecules.

"With these, and just a little extra energy waveguided through your fingertips, you'll open the way for me into any isolated network islands."

Hacking was his job, and he was sure they'd face many obstacles when the security shuts all the doors. *Two minds are better than one.* While the girl was optimized for warrior-caste faps and superfast manipulation of photonic network channels, Nathi's posthuman mind was very good at computation and analysis. They made an odd but perfect match—a man five centuries old and a child.

He didn't want to think about the price.

"What of the pressure?" the girl asked. "The lungs—"

That was the easy part. For both skin and eyes, Nathi controlled the tensile strength of metasilk, which could be formidable. And the lungs....

"No need to breathe. We'll be hermetically sealed."

"IT'S TIME TO LEARN TO BREATHE," HER NANNY TELLS HER. She is in a dancing harness, hovering on her magnetic wings. Her Nanny is a big, warm presence at the blurry edges of her memory. In this one, she is maybe five years old.

"But I already know how!" she protests and starts to puff. "See?"

"No, not that way." Her Nanny's smile is like a fuzzy warmth outside her field of vision. "There is a special dancing breath, for flying. Try to breathe *inside*."

68
LEONID KOROGODSKI

"Inside?" She blinks.

"Imagine that you breathe the air—*prana*—into your legs and arms, into your stomach, down your spine, and everywhere you can think of."

Everywhere? She nods. She closes her eyes. She tries. "It's... tickling. Everywhere."

"Shall I help?"

Nanny is fast. Before she knows it, the girl can only laugh.

5

"NOW FEEL YOUR BODY—ALL OF IT, WITHOUT THINKing," Nathi tells her. "Find your inner self."

But in this dream, she has no other self.

She breathes—or rather, she imagines breathing, trying to direct some *prana* through the brain's internal model of herself—the brain's predictive engine, constantly comparing the real world to the internal model and then readjusting the predictions, binding action and perception in reentrant loops.

Only, the real world is gone, her tiny body lying in a coma outside the dream. And her internal self is held together only through her genie's will. She feels his presence, at the center of her consciousness.

She breathes. She feels it all.

Does he?

THE GIRL HAS PARAHUMAN SKILLS FROM BIRTH, NEW action patterns mere humans only dream of. She must learn to activate them. How?

Nathi knows faps, emotions, and consciousness are like "software optimizations" of the brain's predictive engine that have evolved to handle the complexity of multi-limbed articulated movement. Though robots could be very good at specialized, pre-programmed tasks in a predictable environment, a brain would beat a robot any time in arbitrary, unexpected circumstances, since that's what it has evolved for.

Nathi knows—with certain enhancements of the body and of nerve conductance speeds, one can do things the best of martial artists of the olden times could not *conceive* of being possible—if one performed the necessary movement patterns fast enough, without thinking—if they'd been ingrained as faps.

He knows—those martial artists had to spend long years of repetitious hard work in order to prepare their bodies physically. They had to go through demanding exercises, over and over, in order to entrain new action patterns. Still, no human had reactions faster than 8–12 hertz, the rate at which the brain sends signals to the motor neurons.

But a parahuman brain can be overclocked.

The posthuman mind is modeled after the human brain, while still retaining much of the machine's raw computation power. This is what makes posthuman soldiers so valuable.

But they are still constrained by the digital nature of their minds. Without true pink noise, they do not cope well with unpredictability. And *this* is what makes parahuman warriors so feared.

The girl has got external skills for free. And Nathi has further improved her motor circuitry and muscle structure, primed from birth, and has installed nano-magsails inside her limbs, in metasilk extensions. She is physically able. She can do amazing things—but, it would be like trying to walk while thinking over your every step. She has to learn to liberate her inborn faps. She must let go, let her body flow like a river. Must perform without losing time to think about the routine. Together, they could have both consciousness and faps engaged and shared between their minds.

He has to teach her that. But where to begin? One cannot do that just because one must. He knows faps are triggered by the emotional background. But he can't invent a new emotion by order, can't discover a new state of consciousness like that. The girl must find it for herself, just like the great masters of old had through long years of practice.

Unlike them, she has only two days to master inner forms. Can she?

"**N**ANNY, TELL ME MORE ABOUT UNNIYARCHA. PLEASE?"

"Again?"

Her Nanny is a gentle arm around her shoulder, a voice descending from above her head. She looks straight up—into the shining blur of memory. She's maybe eight. "Again."

"What would you like to hear about? I can tell you—"

"How beautiful she was." She smiles. "Was not she beautiful?"

"She was." And Nanny's fingers lightly brush her hair. "The most beautiful of women, as the ballads say."

5

"But she was also a good fighter, right?"

"She was the best—"

"With her *urumi?*"

"Yes. The flexible sword she kept hidden in her belt." Her Nanny smiles—a warmth from up above. "See? You already know everything."

"Not everything! *Why* did she fight?"

Her Nanny sighs. Her fingers lightly tap the girl's bony shoulder—the fingers that could cut an enemy in half. "She lived in difficult times. Never-ending wars, constant feuds."

"Like now?"

Nanny doesn't smile.

"Was she the same caste as we are?"

"No. Castes were different back then. For she lived very long ago, in the 16th century, in South India. She was the Chekavar caste. Their men were born to fight in the *ankam*—duels to the death to settle disputes for the higher castes.

"The ballads say:

> "One born a Chekavar
> Earns his bread at the point of his sword.
> If anybody comes for an *ankam*
> He can't refuse to go.
> Better far to die with honor
> Than to die a plain death."

Goose flesh over her skin.

"Nanny, did Unniyarcha too fight in *ankam?*"

5

"No. Not everyone must fight and die." Her Nanny sounds wistful. "Unniyarcha had a son. But hey! She had enough adventures of her own. In a fight, she was as fearsome as Kali in *raudram* state. Why, once she fought against the fighters of a rival clan who tried to kidnap their women—and she beat them, single-handed!"

Yes! She claps in joy, but quickly stops. "Like Kali? Does it mean she too was always naked, and she had blue skin?"

"Well, no. If she did, she never would have had to fight."

"What does *raudram* mean?"

"Translated from Sanskrit, it's anger. That is its plain meaning. But it's also more than that." Now Nanny pauses, and the brilliance of memory is dimmed. "One isn't in control when angry, like chaff blown by emotions. One must have mental power to banish doubt. *Then* you fight."

And dance!

"*Raudram* is the kind of fury that only makes others afraid, caught in emotions that make them want to run, the kind that makes the mighty shrivel when facing the small—*before* you act."

"How does it feel?"

മെയ്യ
കണ്ണാക്കുക

But Nanny doesn't speak at once. "Like *meyya kannakuka*, we say in Malayalam. When the body is all eyes."

SHE MOVES—A VORTEX SPINNING IN THE SPACE MARKED BY the angles of her limbs, her body turning, bending, snapping back in flight. Her dancing phrases—a vocabulary of triangulated movement, punctuated with sharp turns. She is a fury transformed, the chaos of the external world turned into a controlled kaleidoscope of movement swirling around the center of her focus—*their* focus. Nathi's mind is shared with hers; he can't but stare deep into the maelstrom—the force of consciousness behind the liberated patterns of her will.

He cannot speak. He understands without words.

These patterns have been churning like an endless mantra while she was in the coma—disconnected from external movement, unrestrained by consciousness. This was the kind

LEONID KOROGODSKI

of space she had been building, with the Fairy's help. This was what the coherent theta brainwaves were about, in truth—just like the theta waves in a meditating master yogi. Activated by Nathi's music. Like a face with an emotional expression, shown to a spaceship pilot to convey, within a single mental image, the essence of tons of data, saving on processing time.

They see without looking.

They are one. Pronouns merge into a single "us"—the shared point of self-awareness, the center of the spinning vortex, spelling their name across the sharp, triangulated space, the name they *know* they will not forget.

"WE ARE THE DANCER."

5

"IT IS TIME."

Who said it first? It didn't matter. They were on the threshold of the merge.

They'd just received the message, via the spy node in the Needle, that the Dragon Guard ships were already in position. Nathi's nanobots were in position too, ready for "magneto-synthesis," to provide energy for their body's cells.

Their body. Yes, today they would join their minds. The girl could not survive without him. Without her, he didn't want to live.

He thought about his backups that still remained out there, in his former order's storage databases. He'd considered erasing them, but that may have attracted his superiors' attention. If the Flamethrowers were right, that might not even have been possible. The posthuman numbers were constrained by hardware; each copy put enormous strain on the resources. Rather than building an army of identical backups, the posthuman-holding orders opted for diversity, injecting new blood with every converted human, looking for the fittest in an e-World variant of natural selection.

For all Nathi knew, they could even erase those they didn't want to keep—perhaps the ones that weren't so eager to continue dying for them in the war. So much for immortality.

5

But he was certain his backups existed. He was too good a brain doctor, probably the only one among the posthumans. How would it feel to later meet himself?

Himself? Not really. For he would no longer be that man.

In silence, Nathi turned to scanning e-World traffic. Almost all of him was now inside the brain and ready to cut off his e-World links.

It was like death—and birth.

We posthumans are a species with "anterograde amnesia," incapable of giving birth to an entirely new mind. Thus we forget our future. If not for a continued stream of human recruits, no new posthuman generation would appear with a brand new vision of the world. *We aren't in your image, Father. Left alone, we would ever be the same old, the same old.*

Perhaps, he wondered, if only they could find some new internal senses no human had imagined—perhaps then they, the posthumans, could create a novel kind of space, a place of their own to call home.

But is it possible to share the internal? Nathi asked himself.

And answered, *How else can one create a work of art?*

He looked inside himself. A strong but gentle feeling of being submerged, not moving, waiting—a potentiality confined.

"Like lying at the bottom of a lake," the girl said suddenly. And Nathi started.

He had not been called by the ancestor shades, the *amadlozi,* like so many of his predecessors on his mother's side. He'd never found the sacred pool of running water by a waterfall. He'd never met the great snake at its bottom, only seen by those called, nor taken the white clay the snake lies on. He'd never seen the rippling surface of a lake when looking from the bottom. He had never risen from the water a new man. Diviner. Wizard. *Isangoma.*

Instead, he'd become an *umkhovu,* zombie. But no one had dug him out of his grave and claimed him, piercing him with a stake. No, he had done it of his own will. It was his choice to be undead, eternal slave to the real modern-day *abathakathi.*

LEONID KOROGODSKI

Would his ancestor shades forgive him, Nkosinathi ka-Xolani? *They always took the accused witches in.*

Nathi looked at the girl's face from outside, through monitors. Nothing betrayed the tension building up within their minds, so close now, at the point of merging. Quiet, like the surface of a lake before a storm. But looking from below....

Their shared dreamspace transformed, the sunlight playing gaily on the surface of a lake, a bare inch above them. Bare microns of untreated skin concealing as of yet inactive metasilk. How far, between their minds?

"Lough-an-Leagh," the girl spoke. "Lake of Healing. The black mud from its bottom cures all the world."

Black mud? Indeed, all things are in reverse in Heaven.

In reverse? the girl said.

So, they already shared the space of thought. *Yes, in reverse.* He gave a mental smile. *Up where shadows are white.*

After today, the two of them would never be the same. It wasn't totally unlike two deaths, one birth. It was the time of their coming out, their *twasa.* For their initiation ceremony, every novice *isangoma* had to learn a special dance. Smeared with medicine and ashes, trembling with their entire bodies.

The confession dance—for every dream they had forgotten. It was hard to learn. He hoped they had done their best.

Will it be painful? the girl asked.

No, not really. Their nerves were sure to complain, all over the body, at the time of their transformation when he activated metasilk and the internal mods. But he prepared to block certain pathways in their brain's anterior cingulate cortex—just for a short time, till he trained the neurons to accept the new reality. Pain wasn't a sensation. Pain was an emotion that came together with sensation. But they could be separated.

We'll feel everything, except it won't hurt.

No, no. I mean the Fairy.

He sighed. What if the Fairy was sentient? And yet, they had no chance without her help. They had to let the Fairy loose in

5

the internal networks of the castle. How long until the Fairy breakout would be neutralized?

Perhaps, she will escape? He tried to smile.

She won't.

5

The girl appeared before his inner eye, in white—an apparition floating above inverted waters, red loose hair streaming. Close as they were already, Nathi found that he missed the distancing aspect of sight.

I have forgotten much, she said. *About my family. But I remember our* bean sidhe. *Among my people, many ancient families are followed by one.*

Yes, Nathi knew what a banshee was. *She warns when someone is to die.*

I know many think that she is evil, but she's not! The apparition frowned. *If she was, why would she cry them so mournfully? She is a friend.*

Like an ancestor shade.

Old stories say she used to visit our world, just like the fairies. These days, she only keens over e-World connections, said the girl. *I heard her once.*

When you...?

She shook her head. *No. Those doomed to die can't hear her.* The apparition reached for him. A touch. *Keep watch for mine.*

He hoped he would not succumb to the temptation not to die—but to run back into e-World, to *live.* For him, to die or not to die would always be a choice. For one last time, he looked at the girl's face through the impassive monitors. Serene. While outside their locked room, the castle—their high-tech prison—waited, quiescent.

The first few milliseconds may decide their fate.

A brief scan, final checks. He had injected some water just below their skin, in preparation for the trip. He'd also left a few backdoors in the control equipment of the transport tubes. It was his job to hack their way around electronic obstacles.

Leonid Korogodski

He wondered if any posthumans guarded their prison, thinking this was just a game. What would they think he was, a zombie breaking with its masters? An escaping revenant?

He sent a signal out, "Entering phase one," and gave the final orders to the nanobots, initiating their transformation.

Time to dance.

Sina, sangoma! he said. *Sina, kubengathi awukaze wasina maphambilini.*

Dance, as you have never danced before.

Their breathing stopped.

In front of monitors, the girl in a coma opened her eyes.

5

6

EVEN AS A HUMAN, GILLES WAS CURSED WITH THE PECULIAR ability to feel the angst, despair, pain of others as his own. So while the other posthumans flocked to rollercoaster sims like *Apocalypse* or *Relativistic Jet Ride,* thrilled by the sense of danger while remaining safe, Gilles spent his quality time in a torture chamber.

Fortunately, there was not a dearth of volunteers. Knights and wizards, dwarves and fairies, gnomes and elves of various persuasions—all were bent on purging evil from his dungeon. This ancient anti-hero game was Gilles' favorite. Rediscovered about a century ago by software archeologists, *Dungeon Keeper* had received a substantial facelift in e-World—from an archaic 3D emulation on a flat screen, it was turned into a full-immersion sim world with five senses, with an omnipresent Hand of Evil and distributed attention capabilities. *The Dungeon Keeper World 3000.* The nature of gameplay, however, stayed the same. The player had to build a virtual dungeon and maintain it, populating it with goblins, trolls, and other evil minions, laying traps.

Defending from intruders.

But if the other keepers played for dungeon-building and developing communities of minions, Gilles' inclinations lay

6

elsewhere. His current dungeon was a pre-constructed one. His in-game "Mentor" told him it was called the Dragon Nest. On his own, Gilles would never have designed a gem like this, with self-repairing walls, magic traps with limited intelligence, and a maze of tunnels snaking in all three dimensions. With Gilles' tacit encouragement, his minions quickly formed broom-racing teams. That kept them busy—and improved emergency response.

What kept Gilles busy was another story. It only took so long for posthumans to get bored and move to something else. But Gilles had discovered the secret of replayability. For in his torture chamber, he was always having a unique experience.

He pulled on harpoon strings. Suspended and spread-eagled in the air, the delicate, pale body of a captive fairy jerked hard, obedient to his commands. Sharp pain from hooks embedded in her bone flared, receded, leaving deep despair as an aftertaste. He shared her fears, the disgust at being a marionette—dejected, impotent. And yet, he knew that he was in command.

It was too sweet.

Gilles always knew which of his visitors were real players, for non-player constructs were predictable. The posthumans, those daring enough to throw a backup away for the experience, made better sport. To them, it was a game of kicking evil's butt—a dungeon romp, save and reload. Strangely, few of them came back for a repeat. Gilles wondered why; they couldn't have remembered his touch. Not one of them had begged him for a save before the end, to keep the memories. He was *that* good.

But this one fairy.... There was something surprising, new about her, so unusual that it took awhile for him to recognize it. Innocence. So rare in the realm of the immortals. When did he lose his? Drowned in the gaps of memory that crept across his childhood....

How does it feel?

Oh, ravishment of innocence!

LEONID KOROGODSKI

He yearned to get beneath her skin. Perhaps, he should have flayed her? No. That would've been too easy, and too fast. Physical pain was boring. And for what—a lifeless trophy? Neh. With post-Singularity technology, he didn't have to settle for a surrogate. He could experience her mental pain directly.

There were advantages in having an omnipresent Hand of Evil. Pressing it against the fairy's beating heart, Gilles yanked on several strings at once.

A ripping sound of the wings torn out, drifting down, like a sharp file drawn across your heart, against the flow of time. Old memories. The smell of sweat, and blood, and fear. Screams. A ripping sound—shreds of nightshirts falling down, as you watch from hiding. An anguished scream of grief for something that's forever lost.

A pure ecstasy.

Her heart—strong, flexile—squirming in his Hand. A yielding, weeping pulse.

A signal from his Mentor. "Jailbreak. Revenant is on the loose."

Time, stop! No such luck. Gilles ordered a high alert.

The broken crypt was highlighted at one of the middle levels—blinking target. "Careful," the Mentor said. "It's dangerous. Bring it alive."

A living revenant? The irony did not escape him. *Nice.* "It won't go far."

Gilles shot his mental presence upward, rolling his awareness like a lining over the walls of tunnels filled with streams of howling, giggling minions. Like the retractable sheath of a launching pad, unfolding. Like an arrow, at one end tethered onto his victim's heart—he clutched it in his omnipresent Hand of Evil. Oh, sweet innocence! *I feel you. You will not escape.* He saw his warlocks speeding up on their brooms, and heard the whistling war cry of steam trolls shooting upward through pneumatic "trollways," felt the specters slipping through his walls, straight through the hard and musty stone. The minions' swarm was rising in a tidal wave through dungeon levels, while his surface guards descended from above, full speed.

6

And way below, far beneath them all, the steady, low beat of Dungeon Heart—the source of all his strength, his life itself—boom! boom!

But what he didn't see was the rogue revenant. *Invisibility spell. Very well.*

His counterspell flooded the tunnels with a liquid light, drawing out and transforming movement. Sliding through the chutes from up above, his fire salamanders floated like blobs of lava in a surrealist coulage. But no trace of hidden motion.

He shut the gates and pushed his omnipresence into high gear. In the three-dimensional cells of concurrent realtime perception—like windows projecting from the center of a dizzying, kaleidoscopic world—Gilles saw the magic doors dissolving into walls and opening false leads. The superficial layers of his consciousness already smarted from the prickling sting of activated traps—

—barbed wire wrapped around the fairy's pale, naked skin. He squeezed, and felt her heart bleed pain into his Hand.

Yes!

"Breach at the Crosshairs Juncture."

He did not require that damn Mentor telling him about scissors cutting through the fabric of his dungeon. He already felt it. His damn dungeon. Anger seethed. He lowered the fairy's feet up to her ankles into boiling water. *Ah....*

"The Eagle's Roost.... The Heron's Pond.... The Pigeon's Mailbox."

Time to shoot.

That's where it'll emerge.

He sped through one of his doors—

—no longer his. The walls around the door blazed with a ring of magic fire; he could not slide past. He pushed his mind against the spell and felt the strength of the enchantment. No simple revenant could do this. *Rival keeper?* And a strong one, too. A small but noticeable chunk of his world went gray in the three-dimensional projections of the simultaneous vision—*claimed*. He couldn't reach it with his consciousness,

LEONID KOROGODSKI

he couldn't help his minions trapped inside. Impulsively, he checked his Dungeon Heart. In no danger? Good. But best of all, he had more than enough mana.

Ha, take this!

The fairy's feet writhed in an agonizing dance.

He uttered the Word. The door exploded before the gust of Dragon Breath. It gave him wings. Embedded in the air, he rushed in. His self-awareness distributed itself across the cloud of blown dust, he saw around and inside himself with millions of tiny eyes. He was the eyes—or eyes within the eyes, looking in myriad directions at the same time, watchful.

Laugh, my wingless fairy! Why don't you laugh? You've lived to see the dark knights fly. In front of him—a maelstrom of limbs and metal armor. An ogre whistled by—and triggered an X-ray Vision trap. It turned him into a bright skeleton, for barely a second. But his black knights' heavy armor kept obscuring the revenant, its movement only marked by bodies thrown to and fro. As indicated by a pile of knights, his warlocks' paralyzing spells worked fine, but not against the revenant.

Gilles sped toward the vortex of an empty space that cut a clear path through bodies of his hapless minions.

There!

No.... He barely licked its shape with thin tendrils of dust before it cleared the obstacle course. But Gilles had it marked. *There!* Sharply edged, a chink of surface—almost two-dimensional, without depth—whirled straight ahead of him. If Gilles had teeth, he would have ground them. His counterinvisibility spell didn't work? The cloud of dust would have to do.

You won't get away.

He found his second breath and chased at breakneck speed after the revenant, inches behind it—as a cloud of all-seeing eyes. All-touching eyes. All-tasting eyes.

Ah, little fairy, you'll be my masterpiece. In three dimensions. *Where is my magic brush?* He plucked the hardest quill out of her torn-off wings and sharpened it. *Blind drawing would be nice.* He poked her eyes out.

6

Ah! A bare hint of contour just ahead, in flight—all planes and angles, a contraption of thin intersecting surfaces, revolving, cutting through distorted space—down, down, down through the tunnels. *Touch* that strange, illusive shape; before it disappears, try to trace another contour line—*where it must hurt.* You'll know if it does. For, at the same time, you repeat the drawing motion with sharpened quill, without looking at the fairy—the art of blind cut. Move with it. You'll know if it works. For if you do it right, more of the dust will catch up with the revenant, marking new contours. *Carve* hachure lines to capture the relief—with light and dark and all gray areas of shadow. Then cut again.

And bleed the edge.

Just like the time you sneaked into the Graduation Ward and watched from hiding, with some other boys who also, as if by command, gathered together at the same time, as your superiors cut "graduated" crèche-sisters, their minds transferred and bodies no longer needed—turning them into the screaming masterpieces of triangulated flesh.

And when you've marked enough, when you're a cloud wrapped around the escaping revenant with tactile multi-angled vision, squeeze it—press it hard to mark its skin over the ghostly bone; like a drawing made on the hard, rough surface of a brick—the real texture of the world beneath a thin veneer of our wishful thinking. Keep pressing, rasping over it with your dusty wind—or simply squish it like a sponge, making wet and dripping splotches over the softness of an innocent heart.

Innocence deserves a ravishment. Because all innocents are fools, dangerous fools. They allow true evil to thrive, out there in the real world—just by pretending it does not exist, or that they cannot be responsible. For no matter how you suppress it, your dark side will always show up.

At least, it's just a game. Out there, in the real world, you'd never hurt a fly. You *know* this.

A game?

It's no game.

LEONID KOROGODSKI

Your masterpiece? It's done. Your eyes are open. You see a human girl, a child. The scenery all changed. From out of the gaping mouth of a transport tube, she's falling through the vastness of a spaceport vault. *Hey, little girl, why fly without wings?* You saw it once already, at the crèche for the test-tube children like yourself, waiting for your mind to finish its development to the adult state, then... ah, immortality just years around the corner! How could anyone then want to kill oneself? Unthinkable!

A beautiful blue sky, no clouds outside their skyscraper—and a girl in flight. Just outside the windows—one blink, and she is far below, gone.

O little girl, why jump without wings?

Why do you have to ask? You see it now; you are free. Your blinds are down—and the fairy? You thought you knew her inside out, drinking in her fear, her angst, her pain. But she's impenetrable. And her heart—a mirror, you have drunk yourself. Your very own self, pretending to be innocent—another posthuman fool, with every other action killing or tormenting people, real people, and protecting those who say "jump!"

That's why all innocence deserves a ravishment.

My little girl, I won't let you fall. I'll help you out.

With an eager smile, Gilles turned his Hand of Evil on his own Dungeon Heart.

6

7

THIN MARTIAN AIR STREAMED AROUND THEIR BODY, HEAT-
ing up at their speed. If Nathi ever wondered what it
must feel like when one's flayed alive, he now knew
it. Skin nerves screamed. But—no pain. It didn't hurt.

Pain wasn't in the complex mix of emotions that nearly
overwhelmed him now—joy and grief, pride and exhilara-
tion, hope mixed with apprehension. And surprise. He didn't
know what to make of the odd pull that kept contorting their
lips—now shared between the two of them. If anything, he
was in no mood to laugh.

His privacy was over.

Too bad, no air for a giggle, the girl thought.

Though perhaps she didn't think in words. He wasn't sure
anymore. They now leaked both symbols and emotions
between themselves.

You'll have to settle for a smile, he thought right back at her.
And he obliged.

Such an amazing thing to move one's lips again, after five
centuries. For real—no simulation, this. And though their eyes
drank hungrily of the amazing world of Martian polar night,
laid open before their night-vision, Nathi also listened to the
song of their body, deep inside.

7

Up in the dark sky, bright blue streaks—the ion exhaust trail of their shuttle. It had given a parting boost to their magnetic wings, propelling them sideways and almost horizontally. They would cover quite a distance before running out of steam.

It was a stroke of genius. Who would have thought back in the castle that the girl would *leave* the shuttle, falling naked into freezing, almost airless space? Just in case, Nathi had hacked one of the smart spacesuits they had discovered inside the shuttle, programming it to pretend that it was occupied. As he expected, no one had dared to shoot the shuttle down in the first few minutes of its flight, without asking their superiors—the girl was much too valuable—while he and the girl had been busy cleaning their skin of that damn marker nanodust, in order to regain invisibility.

Thank goodness that the enemies had weapons all set on stun. The low energy blasts flowed around their polaritonic skin like water. Not so the nanodust. To clean it was a job for nanobots, of exquisite finesse. For even one remaining nano-speck could break their disguise.

It worked. The shuttle was still roaring away—the center, hopefully, of the castle's attention—while they gained more distance, thanks to their good initial gliding speed, enough to carry them across the polar cap. They flew above the branching web of "Martian spiders," their fractal hairlike cracks looking so much like "lightning flowers"—the Lichtenberg figures just like those seen on victims of a lightning strike or in art venues, captured in artful slabs of polymer. A lightning frozen, splayed over the Martian ground.

How can one not marvel at Mars? Both majesty and beauty were in its stark landscapes, wrought by the electromagnetic force but often looking as if made by water—that had fooled so many people once.

O Mars the beautiful! Too bad he couldn't sing.

This leg of their journey didn't take much toll on their energy supply, for they were warm enough at their speed. But, best of all, the Fairy was still alive. She *must* be, for the castle showed no sign of launching orderly pursuit. *What if she's winning?* The girl beamed, and Nathi wondered if more posthumans in the castle joined their side, other than the guard that let them go. Why not attack right now? Why did the Dragon Guard decide to wait?

They soon knew why.

In front of their eyes, the empty shuttle suddenly changed course. At first, it slowed down somewhat; then it turned, bound for the castle. No interceptors had been sent in order to intimidate the non-existing pilot. No warning shots. Somehow, someone at the castle had regained control remotely, had hacked the navigational brain of the shuttle speeding at full power and ordered it back.

Which meant that backdoors had been built into the shuttle, masterfully hidden. Who knew whether the Flamethrower healer wizards had discovered every backdoor in *his* mind?

Nathi knew that there was a Watcher at the castle, recently arrived. A woman who had lost her son, about the girl's age, to the Flamethrowers not long ago, in a prisoner exchange gone wrong. He didn't expect mercy. Watchers, the highest-ranking wizards, had full access to the e-World's layers far below anything a posthuman could perceive. And they had special cyber-faps of their own. Any one of them could wrap the best posthuman hacker around their fingers while *asleep*.

The castle's silence was deceptive. He was certain that the mutiny was over, suppressed so quickly an attacking force would've been hard pressed to use it to advantage. Worse—no posthuman servant, however good, could have disabled the castle's multiply redundant systems. Neither could a Fairy. Not in such short a time.

With a heavy heart, the Dancer watched the shuttle swallowed by a retractable sheath, like a chameleon's tongue darting out of the very same vault they had left not long ago.

So. The conceit was over. The castle knew the truth.

Nathi expected no interceptors, no search parties to sally forth—not anymore. If any had been sent, they were already out, stealthed. But that was not the worst of it. Despair gripped his mind—a still, thin cry.

He knew it was his turn.

7

"ENTERING PHASE ONE."

The ship's collective mind relayed it straight into Naomi's brain, jacked into the ship's polaritonic network. Intercepted by the battle cruiser's self-aware "skin," the signal bloomed into a harmony of synchronous sensations, triggering Naomi's battle instinct.

Because phase one meant the Dancer was already on the move, for at least five minutes.

We imagined you'd enjoy it, the ship said.

Naomi smiled. *Sure.*

"Hell be damned!" Naomi roared over the com. "Ships of the first column, report." Her DareAngel had already forwarded the signal to her second-in-command, Rostam, the leader of the second column.

She initiated the ship's segmentation, feeling her life capsule's separation like a tear in her skin. Pushing the direct brain feedback into the background, Naomi opened her eyes. The wall above her body turned transparent.

Stars. Myriads of them. But she was long past her first crush. She found their target, the red eye of Mars—a tiny disc as seen from far below its south pole.

O my baby. Look what we must do.

But no use dwelling on that. They had to hope that the girl was safe.

The other "stars" around her—the crew's life capsules, tagged with names and vectors of direction, waiting for the ship to recombine, while hurtling all together at the same initial speed of some one hundred miles per second relative to Mars—the speed about to increase tenfold.

LEONID KOROGODSKI

Naomi watched the ship's polaritonic skin turn inside out, going through a reverse metamorphosis from something like a butterfly back into a cocoon. The magsail masts lay out in a spiral around the outside of the enormous hollow cylinder, while the powerful plasma jet engines moved inside.

She latched her capsule back onto the ship and reestablished a direct link. All around her, the DareAngel's crew was settling down in positions on the outside of the ship's surface, ready to split off in microseconds, rescuing a portion of the ship's collective mind, should they be hit.

"The Pearless, all set."

"The Bird of Prayer, standing by."

"The Peregrin...."

Two columns on parallel courses. Never since a certain naval admiral more than a thousand years ago had anyone tried such a risky battle plan. The enemy could concentrate their fire on the leading ships before the task force would be able to respond.

Of course, that meant the DareAngel had to lead. Naomi couldn't ask the others for a sacrifice without going in first.

Don't worry, we will carry you. She winked. *In pieces.*

Ha-ha-ha! We'll have you first!

Naomi laughed. The damn attentions of her crew must have been rubbing off the ship's collective mind.

The envelope of her stress sarcophagus slid over Naomi's prostrate body. She disconnected from her body, totally relinquishing control, even awareness of it—remaining just a naked mind connected to the ship's. She hated this, but knew her human body couldn't cope with the stress that lay ahead. She knew, only if it were immersed in strong paramagnetics and instrumented heavily with nanobots, adjusted at the ship's reaction time, could it survive the crazy rpms of the ship's cylinder.

Could it? No one had tried this method of attack. It was against all military wisdom to attack a highly fortified castle without gaining local e-World superiority—moreover, a place of such importance that, for all intents and purposes, it held

7

the keys to Mars. Yet this time, their combat wizards were engaged in a diversionary action all around the Martian equator. No wizards in the Task Force "Trafalgar." They didn't have the mods for this.

The wizards cannot dance.

They were the Dragon Guard. *They* were the ones who had a crush on Death. They all knew why nobody had returned from Death's embrace—the bastard was just too damn beautiful.

Weather report!

The answer came in seconds. No solar storm yet.

Damn, Naomi swore.

With its eccentric—elongated—orbit, Mars was coming under strong electric stress in the Sun's radial electric field, as it was hurtling into southern spring, closer and closer toward the Sun. The dust storm season. With the Mars–Jupiter conjunction, the plasmatail of Mars was flaring, drawn out more than halfway toward Jupiter. She *knew* that; they had hitched a ride on it.

But—no storm. *Damn. Damn!*

"We'll have to make our own weather, boys," Naomi sent. "The DareAngel—off!"

The plasma engines roared to life, the DareAngel sprouting long jets out the middle of her cylinder, for everyone to see. In just above five minutes, their enemies on Mars would get the telltale signature of synchrotron radiation in the radio range, emitted by the relativistic plasma particles accelerating in the interplanetary magnetic field.

She couldn't feel her body, but the ship obliged to simulate the (grossly lowered) acceleration gee.

The fiends! She loved them.

Ha-ha-ha!

"The Bird of Prayer—wilco!" From the head of their second column.

"The Pearless—right on the tail!"

The next ship, just a few kilometers behind Naomi's, executed a correction glide, accounting for the DareAngel's jets' displacement, so as to catch their jets inside their own cylinder and add their own engine power.

"The Peregrin...."

The ships in both columns streamed, gathering speed—like beads spread out along the common threads of plasma jets, their engines shooting plasma straight through the next ship in the same column, and their collective minds correcting with superhuman speed for any deviation of the jets from their interaction with the solar wind.

It's time. "Umbrellas up!" Naomi ordered.

The magsails' solenoids, wrapped around the ships' cylinders, inflated their magnetic fields, momentum parallel to the direction of the jets—the only possible direction that did not make their ships slide sidewise, and the most difficult direction to maintain. Hitting the magnetic fields, the plasma jets decreased acceleration somewhat. More importantly, those same magnetic fields were strong enough to split the jets, displacing electrons to flow *around* the ships' cylinders, compressing the remaining ion jets to stream *inside*—creating separate electric currents of ions and electrons, inside and out side the cylinders. In seconds, these electric currents grew so strong that the repulsive force between the opposite electric currents overcame attraction of unlike electric charges— blowing the electron jet envelope far away from the ships' cylinders.

Naomi whistled in her mind. *Our own weather we shall make, all right.*

Just then, the Pearless behind her made a point of tying their jets into a knot.

Damn fine magnetic sail control. The captain, Xīng, was so young.

"Hey, on the Pearless!" Naomi called. "What in the fucking hell was that? You leave me 'peachless.'"

"But.... My Dear Angel, that's *your* job."

What! That could not be Xīng; that was his fucking ship. *In blasted hell, my job.*

7

"She says it is her job," her ship confirmed.

Hey! Your job is to keep my body in one piece. I have a mind to use it once it's over. God help them, they all will. *Oh, baby, baby. What have those bastards done to you? What have* we *done?*

"You do it once again—you hear me?—and you'll regret that you were born."

"Yes, ma'am!"

"Godspeed."

7

The men and women under her command had so little time for pranks. Soon, their jets would be too powerful to play games with. Soon, their electron jet envelope would begin diverting ions from the solar wind, making them flow in the same direction. The repulsive force between the opposite, and the attractive force between the parallel, electric currents would then force the solar wind out of the envelope to join the central ion jets—in turn, increasing their strength, thus drawing even more upon the solar wind, and so on until the ion currents roar with the power their initial jets could never have achieved alone. Soon, the lines of the interplanetary magnetic field would bend in spiral shapes. The gyrating ions would be following the field lines—the force-free configuration—which allowed the jets to break the Alfvén limit on electric current strength in space.

Of course, the ships would be gyrating, too. And that was why they had to custom-build the crew sarcophagi.

Don't make me faint after we win, she sent her DareAngel personette.

Don't worry, chief.

Before the ships began to spin, Naomi broadcast to all her battle cruisers, not in words but in archaic symbols from a millennium ago, as a homage: "The Order of Flamethrowers"—no!—"All free minds expect that everyone will do their duty."

She was sure they would understand.

8

POSTHUMANS DO NOT TIRE EASILY. BUT NATHI WAS EXHAUSTED. After their daring escape, after the struggle against the guards inside the castle's transport tubes, and taking over the shuttle, followed by the painstaking task of picking off every bit of marker nanodust, their nanobots were struggling with overload. Between dedicating some of them to their magsails, some to maintain invisibility in both radio and visible ranges, more still to run their "magneto-synthesis," they didn't have any resources left.

Now they also had to block the infrared, to keep from freezing and to hide from infrared detectors. Friction of the air kept them warm in flight, at first. It also made their trail glow in infrared, easily detectable once they had left the halo of the shuttle's heat emissions. If it may have looked at first like just another stray plasmoid from the shuttle's plasma engine, now everyone would know what it was.

They had to split from their original direction, lower their speed, and weave in complicated loops to shake off pursuers—exposing themselves to the harsh temperatures of Martian polar night. No choice but to enable heat containment by engaging their metasilk skin in the infrared. But they could not afford to drop their camouflage in either the radio or visible ranges of the spectrum. Not while they were gliding in the open.

How soon... before we land? he asked.

That was her job; the girl was clearly a better pilot.

About two minutes to that crater. The girl guided their eyes. *Unless you want to drop over flat land.*

8

They'd reached the highlands, on the outskirts of the magnetic field anomaly. Before, they had to run in circles, ending up just slightly west of their original direction.

No. Make for those cliffs. He focused on the section of the rim where "wavy hair" grooves ran down the slope of the crater's wall. *We have to drop invisibility.* Provided that they didn't drop from exhaustion first. But only in the visible, not in the radio range, for the steady surf of e-World traffic beat against their polaritonic skin, demanding entrance—combat wizards. He could not afford the risk.

I hear you. Hold on, doc.

But the landing wasn't soft. The girl was just as beat as he was. They rolled down across the slope in a centrifuge of agony, the ground searing their skin with freezing cold. It was one thing to keep heat from escaping via radiation in thin air, but the solid ground was a better heat conductor. Barely in time, he ordered their nanobots to open the myriads of tiny nano-pores all over their skin, to let the moisture out, from the water he'd injected subcutaneously before the trip.

Thank goodness, it's below −130°C.

The water vapor froze so fast that it had no time to crystallize. In microseconds, they were covered in a microscopic sheen of low density amorphous glassy water.

Patience.

Let it out too fast, and the glass would "hyper-quench," becoming nearly a perfect heat conductor. But at a low rate, it turned into another phase of glassy water, an insulator thousands of times better than thin air. It was already working to protect them, or they would have died on contact. But only a much thicker layer would achieve the full effect, so they had

Leonid Korogodski

to suffer the embrace of cold for a few more seconds. Nathi hoped the exotic glass would hold, for every bump felt like a wrench twisting around their throat.

Nhliziyo yami!

They had stopped, wedged in a narrow deep groove that snaked down the crater's slope. Settled over the same patches of skin, the cold became intolerable. Then it eased.

They lived. As pain retreated, Nathi dropped their invisibility to free some nanobots. Ah, sweet relief!

Pain? That was how Nathi knew the anesthesia of the anterior cingulate cortex had worn off. He did not renew it. Their neurons had adjusted, and—how could one live without pain? How could one grieve?

And how to gauge danger?

A fast shadow skimmed over the crater, covering the stars. The Dancer shrank into the groove. Their skin was now blue from lack of oxygen, showing through the thin layer of glassy water, sprinkled with red Martian sand. They hoped that whoever looked for them would not expect to find a naked girl encased in layers of exotic glass.

They waited.

Nothing.

Then, they felt it. Like the mourning toll—if *you* were swung to strike the bell, and not its tongue. Like deep vibrations of bass music well below the range of human hearing. Below the metasilk's range, too.

Not sound, but a slow pounding against their electromagnetically sensitive skin.

They have a fucking ELF transmitter!

Nathi checked himself. He shouldn't have used foul language. But the girl said nothing. This was no time to dwell on sharing a body with a young girl at the brink of puberty. He knew that she had grown while in coma. Nature didn't wait. But their mutual education had to wait—they both felt the urgency. At their frequency below 30 hertz, the ELF waves penetrated just about anything, including their body, soil, and rock. The

8

Dancer couldn't be located with that, leaving barely a dent in the enormous natural ELF resonator chamber, reaching to the top of the ionosphere. But that was not what the Extremely Low Frequency waves were being transmitted for. Nathi had cut off all their connections to e-World, blocked any contact at radio frequencies. Nothing could force them to accept connection—except this.

The low frequency meant that the signal seeped into their minds extremely slowly. High bandwidth contact was impossible. But, if there was a backdoor left in Nathi's digital mind that responded to a short command, he could be *made* to open the rest of his communication channels.

Damn.

They meant to crack him open. Worse—those waves overlapped the brainwaves' theta range. What if they had installed a similar backdoor in the girl's analog brain, too? She showed the signs of relaxation into a hypnotic state. Or was that drowsiness simply from fatigue? Well, Nathi could fight either; he knew how. But he couldn't help himself.

The dastardly command kept seeping into their minds like the susurrus of a magic incantation. How long before the phrase was finished?

Think!

He looked for spare nanobots, tried setting them in oscillations in the ELF range.... Pointless. Their body made a poor ELF transmitter, metasilk or no metasilk, much less a jammer. Worse—they couldn't stay too long inside the crater, either. Their energy reserves were inching slowly into red. They had to reach the Needle to recharge.

Fight them.

The girl spoke quietly, but their shared mindspace reverberated with a calm force.

Fight? he said.

We have to. Or we will never be free—always in hiding. We can beat them—you and I, together. Open yourself, and let them come. She focused their eyes down the slope. *Look.*

T HEY FOUND HER SPRAWLED ON THE CRATER'S FLOOR, FACE to the stars, just a few steps beyond the bottom of the slope. The hardest steps of all—out in the open—but they knew that they *had* to make them.

8

Her ferromagnetic ferrofluid armor remained solid even after these three years. Though burnt in many places, with deep gouges cut into its black spiked surface, the suit was whole. Its integrity was never compromised. Nor did it fail to shut its heat protection down in the event of death. Intact, her Nanny's frozen face stared at them with open eyes—crystallized, the luster of anthracite.

No, it was something else that killed her.

Interfacing with her suit, they probed its "black box." The smart suit's circuitry was working still. The records were intact. She wasn't shot, nor did she fall down to her death. She died in flight.

Asphyxiation, Nathi said. *She ran out of oxygen.*

It should have lasted her a long, long time. Enough to reach the nearest Flamethrowers base.

But she promised to come back.

Or to die trying.

It wasn't hard to see what must have happened. She had called for help, held off the enemy before the Needle, and then tried to take the castle back. A desperate attack. No, several. Her suit's records showed she had recharged nine times at the Needle and was on her way back to the front when—

Nathi imagined what it would be like to go back into a hopeless fight, over and over again, just as you knew your oxygen was running out, as you felt life leaving, as you gasped for breath—yet kept on going.

He suddenly was struck by how alien the very thought of breathing had become. And yet, they may still die, if they ran out of energy—same as Nanny.

Look, her Dragonclaws still have some charge, the girl said.

8

Bending over her Nanny, she unfastened Dragonclaws from a lifeless left hand. Several blueberries rolled out of the palm, with tiny fragile stems—unbroken.

She kicked the armored corpse hard. Pain blossomed in her naked foot. *Damn you.* This wasn't a good time to let the tears flow. *You were sworn to kill me!*

Thank you. The girl bent to kiss her Nanny one last time—two lips against the helmet's fiberglass, over unblinking eyes. *I will return, to pick the blueberries.*

She took the other claws and armed herself. Too large in size at first, the wrist harnesses shrank down to fit snugly over a child's hands. The laser waveguides wrapped themselves around both arms to reconnect between her shoulder blades to the charger column. *Sorry, Nanny. I'm a better model.*

The girl waited. Nathi knew for whom. A child no longer.

The ELF pounding against his mind grew more insistent. Soon, the "incantation" would be over and he might lose any advantage of surprise. He marveled where had their exhaustion gone.

She fought until her final breath, he said. *Would we do any less?*

Her mental image smiled. Her lips of glass stayed frozen. *No point to hide. They'll find us anyway, from radio transmissions.*

Not if I send them out with different delays in different directions. He smiled back.

You'll have your hands too full for that. Besides, they may have found us already.

True. At least, without having to maintain invisibility, he had more nanobots at his disposal. More computational resources.

They may try to lead me, he said. *Like, you know, back when....* At the spy node, when he went "sleepwalking." He may hallucinate again—they'd make him.

But this time, I won't leave you, she said. *I will guard your back.* She turned one of her claws to point right into their eyes. *Should it go ill,* she said, *you'll never be a slave again.*

He opened himself—

102   LEONID KOROGODSKI

8

NAOMI RODE A STORM OF HER OWN CREATION, ASTRIDE a current of hundreds of megaamperes, singing. Jacked into the ship's awareness, her own body given over into the DareAngel's care and her senses switched over to experience the "body" of the ship, she felt the thrill of a plasma river washing over the screen of the magnetic fields, the ecstasy of channeling a raging stream of energy that roared inside her, through her.

Outsiders—from civilians to Fleet officers from outside the Dragon Guard—asked her sometimes who had it worse in battle, they or their ships. Some of them thought that it was cruel to subject a self-aware being to a much higher risk of losing at least part of their mind. The others said, at least the ships had higher chances of survival, as long as one of their crew comes out of the fight alive. But all of them were answered by silence. In the Dragon Guard, they never thought about it in those terms, both crews and ships alike. Instead, they never settled on who had it best, the crew experiencing the ships' bodies or the ships experiencing their crew's. But how do you put that to an outsider?

Obvious, the DareAngel said. *You have it best, this time at least.*

The DareAngel had a point. This ride was the roughest they had gone through—and the most exciting. Jacked into their ship's brain-grid, she felt the strain of computational demands as something stretching, pulling on the DareAngel's "skin." The other ships down the line had trouble staying on the tail. Some time ago, their columns' envelopes reconnected, leaving ion currents running side by side, aligned with the magnetic field. Now a short-range repulsive force was added to the long-range attractive force between the parallel electric currents, keeping them apart—yet turning around each other, twisting in an ever tighter braid.

Their two columns turned into a double helix.

The DareAngel's navigation fields suddenly jumped in disarray. Naomi smelled the danger level rise like a sharp sting of leather burning.

LEONID KOROGODSKI

Shit. "All ships, wizard attack alert." They would hear her, if their communication channels held. "Experiencing minor noise from wizard interdiction here. Over."

Answers came, but weak and almost unintelligible at times, disrupted by the ion currents' hum as well as by the enemy. Naomi readjusted their control scheme, shifting the load emphasis away from the ship's binary intelligence to their human crew, their brains directly plugged into the ship's grid. The incredible complexity of navigation through this maelstrom of plasma, mixed with challenges of networking defense, flared up with all the richness of the ship–crew shared perception.

Time to dance.

She now had a body in her virtual perception, every movement linked to flight controls, with vision used for targeting, smell standing for the tactical sense, touch for managing redistribution of resources—the crew's consciousness virtualized, contributing their share of brainpower. A single human consciousness could not react much faster than once every hundred milliseconds. When overclocked, a parahuman mind was at least ten times faster on the conscious level, but much faster yet in pure faps. A well-tuned crew of an intelligent ship, with their personettes "zigzag-interlocking" their minds at the full speed of dedicated digital controllers, could react in microseconds.

Best of all, the parahuman minds were harder nuts to crack.

An Alfvén wave down the ion stream ran electromagnetic shudders over the DareAngel's skin. One of the ships in Naomi's column must have lost bearings and, for a fraction of a second, brushed the ion stream at a wrong angle, slow to adjust their magsails. A glancing shear off their magnetic fields—and they popped out of the column like a cork from a champagne bottle, half of their magsails burnt.

Naomi felt the wave as an electric shock. Her vision blurred.

She moved to compensate, exulting in the superhuman nimbleness of her virtual body, felt it merge with movements of the crew—a many-armed and many-legged beast. A flick of

8

eyes to scan the weather data felt like focusing on something that some part of you already had in mind, applying yet another visual push to the same point in the shared field of their virtual perception. Far from having dozens of conflicting efforts pull the ship apart, this actually made the individual errors much less costly, averaging the results—provided most of them did the right thing.

8

"Weather data, compromised," came from the lost ship, and she recognized the signature—the Pearless.

Oh, Xīng. She noticed, from far away, the tails of Scavenger class fighters launching. "Weapons?"

"Intact."

But not maneuverability. Not with just half the sails. Still, even crippled, any Dragon Guard ship could do lots of damage to a swarm of Scavengers. The Pearless already started morphing from the cylinder into a dogfight rigging stance.

"Good luck," she sent.

They couldn't spare anyone. In truth, they were less mobile than the Pearless, because they had to keep the course. She wondered how soon the enemy would realize that.

She transmitted to the others, "Keep the course!"

Checksum exceptions, tasting bitter—someone hacking their weather data. Muffled screams—faint echoes of compulsion resonating through their internal net. She tightened the rollover schedule of their communication frequencies and protocols.

Fuck you. Is that your worst?

The blasted wizards must have lost their punch. No knockdown like the last time, in the botched Horseshoe Ambush, when they had lost communications and a quarter of the Fleet's task force, including the complete loss of two Dragon Guard ships covering their retreat. But now the plasma storm itself made for a fairly good screen.

Unless there was something else to keep the wizards busy.

Mars had grown in her view. Down below them and straight ahead, Naomi saw thin columns of dust devils spawning all around the polar cap, straining to reach up and join the storm. But some were veering toward the power needles, which were drawing on the electron jets.

Are you safe? She hoped that the Dancer had already reached the Needle.

But it was the smaller patch of sky above the castle, at the very edge of Martian ionosphere, that called on their crew's attention—shining at all frequencies on the ship's scanners. That was where the electric currents drawn by their jets passed through the double layer sheath that separated ionosphere from the interplanetary space.

It was a fundamental property of plasma to "coagulate" around any solid body, similar to blood plasma—the very property that gave plasma its name. The double layer sheath contained most of the voltage drop. Within that narrow space, the electromagnetic forces now pinched the plasma braid like a curtain at the waist. Squeezed into a small elliptical sump by the magnetic pressure of converging currents, the trapped plasma at the center pulsed like a beating heart, expanding and contracting, dancing to the rhythm of competing forces.

Damn. Not tight enough. Too bad, no solar storm.

That patch of the magnetopause erupted suddenly, an image of a leering gargoyle tearing through it as though it were paper, in a cheap demoralization trick. *Yeah, right.* The combat wizards doing this were likely sweating over their shut eyelids, trembling. Shared with the entire crew, this image of the struggling wizards did the trick. The gargoyle was dissolving. In its place, she noticed faint traces of two interlocking, spinning teardrops—a budding mini-galaxy.

How long?

The DareAngel showed her the latest calculations. The ships would have to begin braking soon with their magnetic sails, unless they wished to smash into the castle at top speed—which meant they had to disengage the jets and hope that the plasma storm had gathered enough momentum to keep going.

8

"All ships, maintain your course," she ordered. "And add some steam to those sails."

She juiced their magnetic sails up to the limit, felt them strain—both braking and accelerating at the same time. Just a little more, and their material would "boil" with small magnetic vortices—the superconductivity breakdown. If that happened, they could lose their magnetic wings entirely. Few dared to "steam the sails" so close to the boiling point.

8

She shrugged. They were the Dragon Guard.

In five more minutes, their leading ships would be within range of the granddaddy stationary batteries of the castle's defense. At least, there was no question whose guns had the longer reach.

LEONID KOROGODSKI

9

YOUR NAME IS NATHI.
So dark....
Small specks of light respond—flashes of color, vortices, a tunnel with light at its end—triangles sparkle randomly,
then reappear, recombining in the imagery generated by the
mind's internal workings.

Then, a quiet sound enters. Then, patches of skin sensation,
smell. A new world is being created all around you, and centered on you, in a cacophony of random couplings.

Then it stops.

It's dark again. You aren't whole—you don't feel your arms.
You're mostly a naked mind, with skin and, oddly, legs. But you
don't care. You are used to that. You're posthuman, and your
name is Nathi.

Darkness crowds you—a myriad of tendrils reaching out
from every direction to lay claim on your skin. You can't see
yourself. You only feel—a musky smell; tendrils of darkness
whispering all over your skin; slippery wetness probing the
arches of your feet.

Where am I?

You feel a sense of urgency. A beat begins, reverberating
through the darkness, pulsing like a giant heart—but outside

9

your space, which starts contracting and expanding, urging on. You are inside a womb. You didn't have to breathe before, but now you're in want of air. Darkness smothers you. You must escape—escape, immediately!—out of this body of a woman, find the light.

You run—and slip over the wet, cold stones. As you break the fall, as you instinctively discover arms, the stinging water brands you, nails you to the ground as with an electrical discharge at all four points of the rectangle—hands and arms. You scream.

A shaft of light.

You rise. You're in a cave. From a small opening above you, a surprisingly white light falls over the surface of an underground pool. You are enveloped in a symphony of smells—of earthly smells. This can't be Mars.

The surface of the pool begins to glow from beneath. The liquid light reveals strange pictures on the walls. Alien images, half people and half animals. You recognize them. You are touched by the deep sense of antiquity. You've seen them once before, when you visited the land of your forefathers back on Earth. Those rock paintings had existed long before the Nguni, the ancestors of the Zulu, had set foot near the Drakensberg massif—the "Dragon mountains"—back when the land belonged still to the San, the olive-skinned aborigines.

You have a sense of superhuman power awaiting at an arm's reach.

Enter me.

A voice..., and not a voice. Internal pull. You have been *called.*

I've chosen you, isangoma. *You are mine.*

That's what you're here for. A drop of water falls—a splashing sound, and concentric circles widen over the surface of the pool.

You stare into it—

—and know you're not alone in the cave. There is someone behind you, watching you, watching *through* you—and always from behind. You turn—it follows. You whirl—but cannot shake it off. An *other* gaze. Your hairs stand on end.

You dive.

It's quiet at the bottom. In the strangely fierce light, you see the great *ixhanthi* snake coiled over a patch of white clay. It is from its forehead that the strange light shines. A woman with enormous breasts sits near, suckling swarms of shade-snakes. Every now and then, the great *ixhanthi* spits into the woman, she gets pregnant and gives birth—snake after snake.

You crouch low, grab some of the white clay, rise, and draw long lines of white down your arms and legs, across your fore-head and between your eyes, along your nose, over your chin, down your throat, over your chest—until the navel.

"Now I enter *you*," the great *ixhanthi* speaks—and spits all over you and into your eyes. You cannot see. You scream.

And you wake up.

You're blinded by the bright light and the roar of the thou-sands of throats. You're in an enormous crowd. The sweat of bodies packed together mingles with the stench of fear, and with something else, much worse.

"Witch!" someone screams. And then you learn what your own fear smells like.

But you live. It is a girl ahead of you that someone pointed at. She doesn't have the time to say a word in her defense. Fists swing, and the girl's head bounces back to hit you on the nose. You taste blood. The girl's body sags against you, but she is picked up and carried over the heads of the dense crowd. You hear clothes ripping, but you cannot see. You're pressed against the iron fence by a piling mass of bodies, now "promoted" into the front row—forced to watch, your face against the iron bars. Beyond this fence—a narrow open space, then a concentric fence, and then.... You see the girl, stripped naked, pushed into the inner circle, with a tire filled with gasoline around her neck and arms. A flash, and she joins all the other human torches in the circle, wreathed with necklaces of flames—try-ing to run, colliding, falling, screaming, rolling over the ground.

9

The unlucky girl's trajectory throws her smack into the inner iron fence, across from you, and she stays there, upper body forward, blindly pushing with her weight, her burning head stuck in the fence between the bars. Just barely six feet away from her, and face to face, you watch the hungry flames lick out her eyes, shrivel her lips from over the bone of her jaws, and slip inside her throat, stifling screams.

You smile. You *must*. It only takes but one... not even testimony, merely just *one finger* to point at you. This is what killed the girl. The crowd doesn't call for lawyers. So you smile. Here, in the damn front row, where you are *seen,* where the very iron fence you're pressed against gets so hot that it can leave a burn—here, you smile. And make it better than the girl has done.

When is my turn?

You look around—everybody does, to look for enemies—if not to point at, then to see who would be first to point at you. And if you do find someone..., then *you'd* better be the first. You've seen the kindest neighbors here break and point in terror at whomever they have scolded once for broken windows.

You have a woman's breasts. You're in the body of a woman and, beyond doubt, deep inside, you know that you possess your own mother's body, that you are inside your own mother's mind.

Across your chest—two *iminqwamba* leather strips, draped in the shape of X. The ancient dress of a diviner, *isangoma.* You have never worn it other than on ceremonial occasions. But this time, knowing that you could not refuse to come—that would've been suicide—you've put it on, afraid to be mistaken for a witch. For who else could have done it, if not *izangoma,* the enemies of witches? A sudden fear strikes you—who if not a witch? You now regret you haven't worn only one strip, to look like an apprentice—less conspicuous. You check yourself—has your facial expression changed? The other faces, pressed against the fence around the circle, smiling, laughing,

LEONID KOROGODSKI

looking just as frantically around as you do. They swim before your eyes. You're terrified.

Who but a witch?

You have to get away. You *must.*

You try to push back through the crowd—a mistake. A man behind you starts to yell, "A—"

You are quick. A punch into his jaw, upward with all your strength, and, "—witch!"

He drops unconscious, and in this dreadful noise, who is to say who was the first to cry? He is a big man. Gathering him up takes time; a path is briefly opened before you through the crowd. You escape in the commotion, and when you're far enough from the front rows, you just elbow your way, not caring what anyone would think, not caring if you would have to hide forever after this.

Hating yourself.

You run.

Across the squares peppered with ashes, down the roads flanked with rows of stakes, the people on them turning their heads to stare at you, their lips combining in a soundless, "A witch. Witch. Witch...." Their fingers pointing.

So you run. Ahead of you, a fiery procession, blazing—burning people dancing, heading straight at you. You turn—it's right in front of you. You whirl—but cannot shake it off. The burning cadavers are laughing, pointing their arms at you, "A witch. Witch. Witch."

You recognize their leader—that's the man that you made burn. "Your man, I am. Your man, I am," he says. "Now give your man a kiss." He opens his mouth, and inside—a darting tongue of flame.

You dart aside. You must escape. Escape. Escape.... Must run away, away from all these horrors. Out of this city. Out of this body. Out of these memories, this dream.

A dream?

You've stopped before a stream. A ford. A woman with red hair and white skin, bent over her work. The woman's washing

9

something. Heads. Severed heads. One of the heads speaks up. "Go no further."

And a little girl's head adds, "For if you do, someone will have to stick you through the eye."

You blink. That doesn't make sense. But you feel vague stirrings in your memory. The heads..., they look familiar.

"Don't you recognize me?" the first head says. It's your father's. "Now, sonny, what're ya doing there in my wife?"

He stares, and you lower your eyes, ashamed.

"Don't be afraid, don't be afraid. We are your sisters!"

"We're your family," a woman's head says, and you recognize your wife. Her sudden death had made you think of immortality. Her eyes leak blood. "We miss you dearly. Don't be afraid."

"Come out to play, come out to play!" Dark braids sweep through the dust as the girls' heads jump up and down.

"Join us."

"Don't forget your promise."

Promise?

"The decapitation game!" Your father's voice is always young. "Remember? You have cut our heads first. Now it's your turn."

"Your turn! Your turn!"

You back away.

"You don't remember?" Your mother's co-wife looks so sad.

"Unfair! Unfair!" your half-sisters cry. "We've got no arms."

You don't remember? Don't remember? Don't remember?

Piles of skulls.

"You don't *remember?*"

"I can help," the Washer-at-the-Ford says—and lifts her face.

You run. Back to the burning grounds.

A hymn to the goddess of death Kali, by Ramprasad Sen (1720–1781).

In the marketplace of this world,
the dark mother sits flying her kites.
One or two in a hundred thousand
snap the string and fly away bondless,
and how she laughs, clapping her hands!

LEONID KOROGODSKI

He found her, this time as Kali, back at the empty burning grounds, sitting on the ashes. Darker than night, naked but for a garland of skulls and a skirt of severed limbs, with baby fetuses for earrings—flying her kites.

He didn't run away, he didn't shake in fear, but he looked Death eye to eye, unflinching. Then and there, bowing his head onto the chopping block, he made her laugh.

9

THE SKY WAS BURNING IN THE NORTH. A TINY STRIP OF color, but it was enough. The polar night was over.

I would have lost without you, he told the girl.

Brains are harder nuts to crack. She smiled.

Pink noise.

He'd never have admitted it before. He used to think he was the savior, that it was he who selflessly stepped in to fill the broken part of the girl's mind. He had never thought that she would fill a broken part of himself.

Well, that was tough, she said. *You didn't want to let me in, at first.*

Nathi was glad he did. *I never thought that I could break my bonds just by accepting death.*

Then welcome back into the human fold.

Could his mother have survived? Could she have become posthuman, too? He didn't know whether to rejoice or to lament. Probably, both.

But if the memories were true, he knew one thing. His mother didn't choose conversion out of fear. She simply knew she had a hell to pay.

He also knew that, should they meet, he'd help her learn to make her own choices once again. He owed her that much—his life, his memories, ancestors. The pink noise.

But he must also help the others.

Tiny specks of dust were rising from the crater's floor around them in tendrils—up, on spiral trajectories. A storm was coming. High in the sky, and shining like another sun—the teardrop wings of intense aurora locked into a fast-revolving Yin-Yang symbol.

Time to fly.

They primed their magnetic nano-wings, preparing to ride the storm. Yes, they were late in coming into the protective safety of the dust storm front curtain forming around the Needle. But they had a fighting chance to hide within its "Faraday cage" folds.

Illumined by the sunlight, several shapes appeared above the crater's rim. They were surrounded on every side. InsectiEye destroyers. Nathi didn't think they would have their weapons on stun this time.

The girl activated the polaritonic covers of the Dragonclaws. They turned invisible.

It's my turn. Nathi grinned. *We'll have to become twice the girl you are to beat these bastards.*

The last things he felt before he gave up all of his resources —awareness itself—was the vertiginous acceleration as they spiraled upward from the bowl of the crater, and the shattering of glass from over their reactivated metasilk.

*C*OME ON!

Naomi didn't have time for a longer speech. Nuclear mini-missiles came at them in narrow, dense fields of automatic fire, locked on their target.

"Keep the course!"

The DareAngel speared ahead at hundreds of kilometers per second, pushing a paraboloid halo of explosions, their defensive lasers searching for nuclear bullets. Even those passing on the sides were dangerous—they were too "smart" to flow in straight paths.

Naomi danced in her ship's body, her eyes darting—targeting. The DareAngel's crew had redeployed their integrated minds to the peripheral anti-missile defense, working together like they shared the body of the ship. But even though they swept their laser beams so fast they covered most of the area ahead of them in microseconds, their lasers couldn't keep their destructive power sustained on maximum for long. They had to make the lasers' every full-burn count.

118   LEONID KOROGODSKI

It was like waterskiing at high speed, trying to catch the drops of water all around you—and staying dry. It didn't help that radiation noise masked the mini-missiles' trails. But the abundant radiation from the many tiny nuclear explosions around them kept feeding their plasma jets.

Come on. Naomi clenched her virtual jaw. For the pain kept coming.

Damage to the X35B group of integration nodes—burning on her tongue. The laser battery on her left virtual forefinger down to 19%. The first crew casualties—

She felt each injury like needles piercing her skin—the ship's crew like a many-armed and many-bodied dancer, keeping on under a shower of arrows, on wounded limbs—a violin with breaking strings—

—a juggler with blind spots.

Naomi heard an echo of a wizard's laughter, sinister and triumphant, as if from far away; felt the stinging bite of arrows that came as if from nowhere. They had lost all contact with Rostam's ship. The same storm that shielded them from wizards now enveloped them like an impenetrable wall. They were the blind eye of a hurricane.

Good. Just a little more. As long as their engines worked.

"Keep. The. Course!" She hoped she was heard. *Just keep the course.*

She listened to the music of Langmuir waves driven by lasers through the plasma.

Just a little more—

She didn't notice the explosion that knocked her out.

When she came to, she was whirling through open space in her life capsule.

Propulsion unresponsive. I am sorry, chief.

Her DareAngel personette using a singular pronoun wasn't a good sign.

How many? she said.

She had suffered a minor concussion and her realtime rad-cleaners had overloaded. Although charged particles

9

were mostly deflected by the ship's magnetic fields, there was much less that could be done about gamma-ray and neutron radiation from the nuclear explosions.

No matter. She had had it worse.

Survival rate of 46%, at least. From what I can detect. You know, they're hiding.

9 True. Sharp burning pain, as if a thin hot poker the size of a nano-needle ran a zigzag scan over her skin—one of the castle's battle lasers hunting for survivors. She was lucky to escape between its full-burn pulses. *Whew.* That was a close call. She narrowly escaped Lord Nelson's fate.

The world was bouncing up and down till she synchronized the virtual displays. Her stuck magsails had carried her way to the north, now spiraling toward the power needles. Far behind her, she could barely detect evasion traces of the crew's life capsules, scattered by the emergency ejection.

Worry not—she checked her shielding frequencies—*we'll piece you up in no time.*

And, like a mantra: *Stay the course. Just stay the course.*

Naomi knew the Dragon Guard would hold.

The castle's missile batteries kept firing into the growing striated funnel with a desperation only equaled by their missile supplies. Above them, the plasmoid at the center of the mini-galaxy pulsed like a heart, compressed between converging spiral arms. While down below, at the base, where the funnel's gaping maw flared wide around the anti-plasma shield—like jewels framed with the bright silver of the polar cap the castle rose, glorious in shimmering, almost translucent beauty. Plasma trails of escape shuttles ran away from it in all directions—rats abandoning the ship. Above, the sky sang in all waves of the electromagnetic spectrum, the shining plasma column turning like a giant drill aimed at the anti-plasma shield.

But this was not what stole her attention. Spiraling around the Pincushion, the dust devils merged into a single front of billowing electrified dust—a Faraday cage, better even than

LEONID KOROGODSKI

the castle's cage that could withstand the electromagnetic pulse from major nuclear explosions—still growing, still reaching upward, higher into space.

And at its rising crest, she saw—no, not a girl—a vortex of destruction wrapped around an invisible and fierce presence, spinning, changing faster than Naomi's virtual displays could catch—and hopefully faster than the targeting devices of InsectiEye destroyers. Some of them were down. She saw shards and pieces tossed about by the storm, the forming and dissolving eddies in the wide-field plasma nets cast over the area by the remaining three, could almost feel the strain on their computational resources.

Then, she noticed a sudden change in their strategy and realized why they grew bold. The Dancer was no longer shooting back.

Behind Naomi, the attack was nearing the critical point.

"Xīng!" She yelled out into space, oblivious to danger. "Xīng!" *If you are still alive....*

I T HAPPENED JUST BEFORE THE ACTIVE NUCLEUS OF THEIR MINI-galaxy accumulated enough power to discharge its jets. The Dragon Guard ships suddenly reversed their engines in a powerful combined thrust, sending a stream of plasma down, straight into the pulsing heart of the plasmoid—and then swung the butterfly wing sails across the stream.

Thrown out of the funnel, they watched that plasma reach the nucleus, short-circuiting the gaps of high magnetic pressure separating the plasmoid from the mini-galaxy's two spiral arms. Confined within the funnel, the electromagnetic pulse absorbed the released energy. At nearly the speed of light, it pierced the castle's anti-plasma shield and smashed through many feet of the protective Faraday cage layers in the walls.

The castle died.

In an abruptly eerie quiet, the Task Force "Trafalgar" dispersed in a rosette above the castle, braking in a horizontal flight. Darkened, grown heavy like a corpse in its suddenly material substantiality, the castle watched with the dark empty sockets of its observation bubbles as the ships wheeled back and thousands of tiny stars—the Dragon Guard invasion force—landed unopposed, claiming for themselves the keys to Mars.

The Order of Flamethrowers was back.

T HEY ROSE AT THE CREST OF THE DUST STORM, ONE STEP ahead of its unrolling spiral "staircase." With all their indicators in the red, Nathi himself was now teetering on the edge of coma. The charge in their Dragonclaws had run out long ago. **9**

Hold your breath. Just hold your breath.

She hardly heard him, wasn't looking back. She didn't see the last InsectiEye destroyers crash, cut down by invisible light from above. Light as a feather, they were lifting up—the Dancer of the sky, just barely one step above the storm. They rose, spiraling around the Needle—and, where they passed, she saw the flywheels turning faster.

Look! The prayer wheels. They turn. We turn the prayer wheels!

They felt the echoes of the electromagnetic pulse like millions of resonating gongs, like alternating bursts of cold and fire running over their electromagnetically sensitive skin, and as a sudden urge to breathe. Although but a tiny fraction of the focused power that hit the castle, those echoes could still kill them easily.

They lived. With eyes wide open, they entered a tunnel full of light and floated toward its other end—but didn't find it, caught by a magnificent magsail frigate that dove from the sky to shield them, like a mother bird, with half-burnt wings.

10

"G——?"

Had someone just called their name? But it was gone—together with her family.

They opened their eyes. The same familiar shapes of medical equipment hovering and turning around their body. Back in the same hospital room, in their prison.

Captured?

Instinctively, Nathi overclocked their brain. The Dancer shot out of the bed, their limbs primed for a complex fighting sequence—

—to be checked, held briefly, then pushed down.

"G——? I am a friend." The woman's voice did not betray the effort, but her block, though gentle, matched every attempt at getting free—a fluid dance of faster-than-thought movements. "You are still too weak. Rest first—*then* you can beat me."

They relaxed. The woman let go of the block.

"Do you remember me?" she said. "I am Naomi?"

Seconds after they had opened their eyes, the Dancer finally awoke—and saw a woman's face that may have been a fair copy of the girl's own if not for the wrinkles and the hardened eyes. Gray strands of hair were poised to soon overwhelm the flaming red.

Somehow, Nathi felt that he'd already made that observation once.

The Dancer shook their head. The woman's smile was gone. "We won," the woman said. "The Dragon Nest is ours."

It took a moment before Nathi recognized the castle's former name. All of a sudden, he felt tired. So much pain, so many sacrifices.... He was free. They won.

But how many posthumans still remained in slavery?

"What must we do?"

"For now, nothing. You must rest," Naomi said. "Recover strength. You've suffered enough." Her eyes took in the color of the Dancer's skin—the Martian red. "Besides, there is a matter of your many... uh, extreme modifications. Nothing, thankfully, that our healers can't take care of."

"No!" The girl must have surprised Naomi. Nathi, too. "I want to keep the metasilk."

I am a daughter of the Martian soil, she added silently. They both had a sense Naomi would've been hurt to hear that.

"And... we have grown rather fond of our superlens sight," Nathi said. He knew the girl would love hunting for blueberries from orbit.

"That won't be necessary," someone cyber-spoke. "Your new ship has superlens viewfinders."

A wink, a nudge—and Nathi recognized his welcome personette. *Rina!* he sent her.

"Ship?" The girl blinked. *"Our* ship?"

"Your ship." Naomi smiled. "A brand new magsail battle cruiser. An intelligent shapeshifter."

"Guess who asked to be transferred to the new collective mind?" The personette sent them a cyber-smile.

"Happy to have you," Nathi said. "We'll make a ballerina of you yet."

"So *that* is how you have managed to seduce my own personette!" Naomi laughed.

But Nathi was already swept by a cascade of the girl's emotions, her memories. The dream flight in the make-believe

LEONID KOROGODSKI

magnetic sail ship. Then, the real flight with nothing but the metasilk skin between their body and the almost airless cold of the Martian polar night. The magic of the layered terrain, the Laceland, the "dalmatian spots." The tickle of the plasma wind over their electromagnetic skin—

And then it struck him. The girl knew it, too. A *battle* cruiser. They had won a battle. Not the war.

10

THE DARKNESS OF THE MARTIAN NIGHT IS CUT BY PLUMES of glow reaching for the sky. Naomi is alone in an observation bubble, watching the Dancer dance up in the air outside the walls—a metamorphosis of fluid lines, the angles shifting and diverging as the magsails follow the silent music. Theirs is a subtle, deadly grace of armored, armed surfaces. The newborn battle cruiser's outlines keep changing, playing with space like an artist's dream, morphing in flight.

They dance. Far down below, their eyes catch on a solitary figure in a bubble, watching them, a tear sliding down over one cheek.

Who is she? the girl asks. She knows they have met, have talked for hours about something—only she does not remember what.

I think she is a friend. A very close friend, says Nathi.

Good. They can remember friends.

The battle cruiser's faces smile.

They dance.

NOTES

AND

REFERENCES

THE OTHER DESIGN

M Y WORK ON *PINK NOISE* INCLUDED MUCH RESEARCH, exposing me to some very interesting science, which I will attempt to summarize here. We live during exciting times, at the beginning of another major scientific revolution.

Not that long ago, if anyone had asked me what was the greatest scientific discovery of the 20th century, I would have been stumped, not knowing which scientific discipline to favor: physics, genetics, computer science? Now, I wouldn't hesitate a bit before naming Ilya Prigogine (1917–2003) and his discovery of spontaneous self-organization in systems far from equilibrium—because, among other things, it spares me from having to choose between so many worthy scientific disciplines: Prigogine's discovery concerns them all.

To most people, the term *evolution* is associated exclusively with Charles Darwin and biology. Prigogine extended the evolutionary approach to many other fields of science.

H E HAD FORERUNNERS. LUDWIG BOLTZMANN (1844–1906) is well known as the father of thermodynamics. But few know that his intent was to do in physics what Darwin did in biology, to explain the formation and development of complex systems. Boltzmann began by studying not individual particles but large populations of them—statistically.

He formulated the concept of *entropy,* a measure of disorder in a system, and discovered the second law of thermodynamics, by which entropy in a closed (that is, not interacting with anything else) system grows with time. For example, if hot water is mixed with cold water in an isolated vessel, the system (not far from being closed) eventually reaches an internal equilibrium, a uniform state with the same temperature everywhere.

This, however, led to a rather pessimistic scenario for the eventual fate of the universe: the "heat death," a completely uniform state everywhere. No difference, no distinction. No life. This was completely opposite to what Boltzmann wanted to achieve, which led him into deep depression. He had failed. Where Darwin showed how a new species could appear, evolving from the simple to the more complex, Boltzmann only showed development from the complex back to the simple.

But, in a sense, he had succeeded. However pessimistic the results, he demonstrated the *irreversibility* of time. After all, all modern physics, classical and quantum alike, describe the trajectories of particles (classical) or wave functions (quantum) as reversible in time. The equations, both Newton's and Schrödinger's, are time-symmetric. The wave function collapse, widely cited to demonstrate the irreversibility of quantum systems, does not truly explain anything, because it is found outside the formalism of quantum mechanics, in interaction between a quantum system and a classical observer: the quantum system changes irreversibly once it's observed. One can say that the wave function collapse is just another formulation of the paradox of time. The equations clearly say that time is reversible. Yet we know well from our life experience that an egg, once broken, never comes back whole.

Some scientists went so far as to claim that time actually *is* reversible, that we simply don't live long enough to notice this. Presumably, eventually, after some gazillions of years, somewhere in the universe an egg mysteriously comes back whole from some random motion of particles.

It took Ilya Prigogine to complete what Boltzmann had begun and show why the point of view expressed in the previous paragraph is wrong.

I NSTEAD OF STUDYING SIMPLE SYSTEMS CLOSE TO EQUILIB-rium, like everyone else did at the time, Prigogine chose as his subject complex nonlinear systems far from equilibrium.

Simple systems are a natural first step in scientific exploration. They can be exactly solved, expressed in formulas. Their solutions can be taken as an intuitive ballpark, something to expect from a more complex system, at least in a certain approximation. They are well defined, more readily reproduced and, therefore, are more amenable to controlled experiment. Moreover, this is how we tend to design. The vast majority of our technological devices, from antiquity to present day, are simple and as closed as possible, because this makes them manageable, more *debuggable*—in other words, predictable. For it is hard to troubleshoot unruly chaos!

The problem with simple systems is that they are already near equilibrium. No wonder Boltzmann had arrived at the "heat death" scenario.

But systems *far* from equilibrium behave quite differently. To be sure, the entropy of a closed system still grows. But an *open* system can theoretically decrease its entropy by passing some of it to the outside environment, so that the total entropy still obeys the second law of thermodynamics. The incredible thing is that, as discovered by Prigogine, open systems far from equilibrium exhibit a tendency completely opposite to the "heat death" scenario: on average, they tend to *decrease* their entropy, spontaneously self-organizing! Think of this as an unnumbered "fourth law of thermodynamics."

A mix of hot and cold water, when left alone in an isolated vessel, equalizes in temperature. But if the water is continually heated, when it boils, hexagonal convection cells spontaneously develop, the water moving up and down in hexagonal cylinders. Once the heat is removed, the water stops boiling and equalizes. In order to keep lowering its entropy and thus increasing order, a system must remain open, must remain in a constant energy exchange with the environment.

The water cannot boil forever. Nor can an even more complex system, much farther from equilibrium—such as a human body—function forever. Every individual system eventually succumbs to entropy. But statistically, in terms of populations, spontaneous self-organization keeps growing. And so must the energy exchange keep growing. Living systems, for example, exchange energy much faster and through many more channels than non-living matter.

But evolution, understood in the broadest sense as an ever-growing spiral of self-organization, is not limited to living systems. From the fractal large-scale structure of the universe to the formation and evolution of galaxies, to stars and planets, to the geological processes, to life—it's no fluke!—and to the brain and consciousness, to our society and culture and economy, the self-organization keeps growing. And in an *infinite* universe, which is the only truly closed system, this progression can keep going without limit.

Who knows what comes next?

Evolution must be God's design!

This is why Prigogine's discovery is so important. It is universal, encompassing everything. It gives us an entirely new scientific paradigm—a science of complexity—bringing the evolutionary principle into many diverse disciplines in its most general form. Prigogine will be remembered long after most of the scientific darlings of the 20th century have been forgotten.

Murray Gell-Mann (b. 1929) discovered quarks (the 1969 Nobel Prize in Physics). Later, he turned to the study of complexity.

THE SYSTEMS THAT DEVELOP BY THE EVOLUTIONARY PRINciple were called *complex adaptive systems* by Murray Gell-Mann. They, and the complex nonlinear systems far from equilibrium in general, have an important property. Any classical or quantum system can be described in terms of individual particles' trajectories (classical) or wave functions

LEONID KOROGODSKI

(quantum), and in terms of the statistical density distribution function (classical) or density matrix (quantum). For a simple system, these descriptions are equivalent; these systems are reversible. But complex systems far from equilibrium have statistical solutions not expressible in terms of individual particles at all (this is what it *means* to be far from equilibrium). The whole is more than the sum of its parts. And it is these solutions that are irreversible.

It is important to understand that the subject of science is the kind of knowledge that can be tested by experiment. Therefore, the goal of science is not to establish absolute truth—this is impossible in principle, since experiments cannot prove, but only can potentially disprove, a theory. The goal of science is to *approximate* reality, to construct a model that allows one to predict the experiment with reasonable accuracy. Science is not a monolith but a rather loosely coupled set of theories, each with its specific domain of applicability. Classical mechanics, for example, does not apply to very high velocities and very small sizes. Quantum mechanics, being linear, only applies to simple systems (as we'll see shortly), and so on. Theories tend to be replaced after a while with new ones. Much of scientific knowledge isn't absolute.

In this light, the above-mentioned defining property of systems far from equilibrium means that many fields of science cannot be reduced to physics. Studying the behavior of dolphins can't be done by deconstructing them into elementary particles, even if one has an infinite processing power to solve the equations.

This is also why there can be no single Theory of Everything.

What cannot be experimentally tested must be believed in (including the *belief* that God does *not* exist). This kind of knowledge is the subject of religion and philosophy. If neither religion nor science intrudes on the other's territory—which has happened both ways and many times—then they are not in conflict.

COMPLEX NONLINEAR SYSTEMS AREN'T SOLVED EXACTLY—NOT even numerically, in many cases. As described in [18], T. Petrosky, one of Prigogine's students, ran a computer simulation for a system with one star, a single planet, and a comet. He tried to predict the number of orbits the comet would make before being expelled from the system. If the initial coordinates and velocities were rounded to one part in a million, the answer was 757 orbits. If up to one part in ten million, it was 38 orbits; one part in a hundred million, 235 orbits; one part in 10^{16}, 17 orbits. Yet different results could be obtained by different ways of rounding the intermediate results of calculations. Without absolute knowledge and infinite precision in calculation, the comet's orbit was simply unpredictable. Yet no randomness was involved. The system operated under the deterministic laws of Newtonian mechanics.

This is an example of the *deterministic chaos* phenomenon, also known as the *butterfly effect*. As shown by Henri Poincaré (1854–1912), there always exist *chaotic* orbits in gravitational systems with more than two bodies. Chaotic orbits never pass the same location twice yet may approach it arbitrarily close. Therefore, even a slight deviation can make a huge difference later on.

The world may be deterministic, but it is not predictable.

D IGITAL SYSTEMS TOO CAN DEMONSTRATE VERY COMPLEX behavior (see [34], for example). Some are even *NP-hard,* which is a technical term meaning that there exists no better algorithm to predict the system's state other than simply running it through its paces. But a faster system can simulate it sooner, thus predicting it. With complex analog systems exhibiting the butterfly effect, this is impossible in principle.

One can argue that the universe is actually not continuous but discrete in space and time, according to quantum mechanics. But this is incorrect, for only simple quantum systems are discrete. And only simple quantum systems are reversible in time. What we call the wave function collapse is the result of interaction between a simple quantum system and a complex nonlinear system, the observer. Therefore, the quantum system ceases to be simple—and ceases to be reversible.

Ilya Prigogine, thus, restored the arrow of time. No, it's not true that time only appears to be irreversible, as some claim. It is just that our simple systems—our ideal, linear approximations

For the mathematically advanced reader: The spectra of the Hermitian operators representing the physical observables in quantum mechanics are discrete only in certain cases.

LEONID KOROGODSKI

to the much more complex, nonlinear reality—appear to be reversible. The real world is not.

B Y THE VERY NATURE OF COMPLEX ADAPTIVE SYSTEMS, THEY experience events when a small quantitative change brings about qualitative changes of enormous magnitude. Moreover, this is bound to happen to any complex adaptive system, given time: the birth of a new species, cancer, epiphany, economic crisis, political revolution, and so on. In general, this is called a *singularity*.

Revolution is the singularity aspect of evolution.

T HE SCIENCE OF COMPLEXITY IS STILL IN ITS INFANCY, developing a new scientific methodology. Ilya Prigogine was awarded the 1977 Nobel Prize in Chemistry for his discovery of spontaneous self-organization in systems far from equilibrium. Until his death, he was the President of the International Academy of Science. Despite that, his work is relatively unknown outside the scientific circles. Some of the related evolutionary paradigms are well accepted by mainstream science, like Neural Darwinism, for example. Some are still being ignored, like Plasma Universe. (Both are drawn upon in *Pink Noise*.)

The opposition to this view can be found in the stubborn hold on scientists that the universe must have the quality of elegant simplicity, that a beautiful theory just *must* be true. But the ancient Greeks too believed that the orbits of planets simply had to be perfect circles—ending with the devilishly, artificially complex system of Ptolemaic epicycles.

For a brief description of epicycles (and their modern counterparts), see *Galaxies in Plasma Lab* on pages 145–146.

There *is* a beauty in the universe, but not the beauty of a simple perfect form. The beauty of the *natural* complexity—the beauty of a tree, not of a polyhedron.

BRAIN AND EVOLUTION

I N 1972, GERALD EDELMAN (B. 1929) RECEIVED THE NOBEL Prize in Physiology or Medicine for his discovery of *somatic selection* in the immune system of mammals. It was his answer to the question of how our bodies manage to produce so many different antibodies, each geared against a particular invader.

Previously, it had been thought that the blueprints of all antibodies were encoded somewhere and were activated during an infection. But the number of all possible infectious agents that our species has encountered in the past and may yet encounter in the future is so staggering that this assumption strained credulity. Moreover, different people produced very different antibodies in response to the same invader.

Gerald Edelman showed that the immune system works by the evolutionary principle. While any other cell in the body carries the same genes, certain immune cells are an exception to the rule. Their genetic composition allows variation. When a new infectious agent is encountered, the immune system's engine guns itself into a frenzy, busily trying different combinations of immune cells' genes, until a fit is made.

This architecture allows a quick response to *any* invader that may *ever* be encountered. In only a few days, evolution does what may have taken rational design decades to accomplish.

B UT EDELMAN DIDN'T REST ON HIS LAURELS. HE PROPOSED that the brain too works by the evolutionary principle. This was the birth of the Neural Darwinism paradigm in neuroscience.

Evolution manifests itself in the brain in several ways. Firstly, as far as its structure is encoded in the genes, the brain is a product of the evolution of the species—*natural selection*.

A neuron that has failed to make any connection commits suicide by a mechanics called *apoptosis*.

Secondly, in a growing organism, neurons compete to make connections between each other. Again we see how evolution is superior to rational design. Instead of pre-programming a specific rigid structure, neural evolution allows the competition to self-optimize the connectivity pattern. This *developmental selection* ensures that even identical twins or clones would never have identical brains. Yet the randomness is not allowed to run amok; the general, high-level structure of the brain is kept intact—a sort of combination of "free market" and control, honed to perfection over the eons of evolution.

Thirdly, in a functioning brain, neurons compete for a chance to fire; that is, to send signals to other neurons. There are two kinds of neurons in the brain: excitatory and inhibitory. When an excitatory neuron sends a signal to another, it encourages the target to fire in turn, whereas an inhibitory neuron tries to silence its target (whether or not either succeeds depends on the current conditions and a variety of thresholds).

If we only had excitatory neurons, they would have quickly synchronized, all neurons in the brain firing in perfect unison, as pendulums that stand on the same floor influence each other via mutual feedback to spontaneously synchronize their oscillations in a process called *entrainment*. Their clocks begin to tick together. But perfect unison is an extremely simple structure; it does not support complexity. Neuronal oversynchronization is, in fact, what happens during an epileptic fit (*grand mal*); predictably, the person is unconscious while it lasts.

Inhibitory neurons create complexity, by enabling competition. When an excitatory neuron fires to another, it wakes up its inhibitory allies, which try to silence other neurons that

LEONID KOROGODSKI

want to send similar signals. The winner takes all. Moreover, the winner is rewarded further: the firing neuron-to-neuron synapses get stronger, so that they are more likely to win in the future. Synapses get weaker if they don't fire for a while. This process is called *brain plasticity*—the brain keeps modifying itself to get smarter, better at reacting to new situations. This is how, for example, we can learn tasks to such a level of perfection that we can perform them on auto-pilot—learning new faps, getting rewired.

In the brain, massively parallel neuronal ensembles thus compete to deliver the best results, comparing their predictions with the feedback from external action, making corrections. The impression that our brain is "single-threaded" is an illusion, for we only perceive the results of massively parallel computations, like many teams that work on the same task. And if you think that our memory capacity is low just because we can juggle only a handful of objects in our mind at the same time, consider how much information is involved in just one object, taking into account all sensory inputs, not to mention interaction with the object, such that the number of forking paths—decisions made on the basis of the object's properties—can grow exponentially. As Daniel Dennett (b. 1942), one of the proponents of Neural Darwinism, put it in [10]:

> Throw a skeptic a dubious coin, and in a second or two of hefting, scratching, ringing, tasting, and just plain looking at how the sun glints on its surface, the skeptic will consume more bits of information than a Cray supercomputer can organize in a year.

NEURONS ARE NATURAL OSCILLATORS OF ELECTRICAL potential across the cellular membrane. When they fire to each other, they can synchronize, producing what we call *brain oscillations,* or brainwaves.

The random variations, necessary to drive the *neuronal selection,* follow the pink noise distribution as $1/f$, the amplitude (strength) of oscillations being inversely proportional to their frequency. A noise following a more general $1/f^a$ distribution is called *fractal noise,* where the number a is its *fractal dimension.* When $a < 1$, chaos is stronger than order; when $a > 1$, order is stronger than chaos. But when $a = 1$, this is the zone of the highest complexity, if complexity is measured by the number of states that the system can tell apart from each other. In other words, $a = 1$ is when the butterfly effect is most strongly felt. Of course, the higher the number of states the system can distinguish between, the higher the amount of information the system can contain. Pink noise is the most informationally dense noise in the universe.

Once again, the evolutionary process has spontaneously established a perfect balance between order and chaos. On one hand, the oscillations in the brain *must* synchronize, for this is precisely how the inputs from disparate sources combine in order to produce a cognitive event. Yet on the other hand, oversynchronization brings epilepsy, a state of mind when large groups of neurons fire in unison—too simple a structure to sustain consciousness.

In a normal waking brain, synchronization must be transitory. The waking (or dreaming) brain is always in a phase change state, like a ball at the top of a hill in an unstable equilibrium, choosing which way to fall—the state of maximum complexity, driven by and driving constantly the butterfly effect.

I suggest that the idea that we do not need to know how the brain works in order to simulate its functionality, currently prevalent in the AI research community, is misguided. We would do better to learn from the brain.

Until we harness deterministic chaos, we will never create a true artificial intelligence. Let's call this the *neuromorphic principle.*

B UT HOW DID THE BRAIN EVOLVE? AND WHY? NEURONS are extremely hungry, energetically expensive cells, yet the brain kept growing in size, from one species to another. What is the evolutionary advantage of consciousness?

One of the fathers of modern neuroscience, Rodolfo Llinás (b. 1934) proposed that the brain evolved in actively, *purposely* moving organisms in order to predict results of movement. Plants don't move purposely, so they don't need—and therefore, don't have—a brain. Tellingly, sea squirts spend the first brief stage of their lives as actively moving larvae—animals, with tiny brains. But as soon as they find a good place to settle down, they turn into plants, digesting their own brains.

We tend to underestimate the complexity of our movement. If you take into account the number of muscle groups in just one hand, and the number of motor neurons activated every tenth of a second in various sequences, then the number of degrees of freedom in moving just that hand becomes so enormous that a CPU-based computer would need to have a truly astronomical CPU frequency to handle it, and at 100% CPU, besides. Yet our brain performs the task effortlessly, with only a small portion of its neurons, leaving a lot of processing power for other things—like thinking.

The computational power of the brain is staggering. It may not be adding numbers very fast, but as a movement and decision making processor it beats a computer anytime. Robots can be programmed to perform well, with repeatable precision in predictable environments. In contrast, the brain never repeats itself exactly, thanks to its evolution-driven architecture. But, for the same reason, it is capable of reacting reasonably fast in *any* situation in various environments that the members of the species may find themselves in over many millions of years.

Faps—fixed action patterns—and emotions are certain *necessary* "optimizations" of the brain's predictive engine. Consciousness is necessary to survive in an unpredictable world, taking over from the auto-pilot when something unexpected happens. Thus, neither emotions nor consciousness are limited to humans. Many animals must have them simply to be functional. I suspect that our first AI children will be more ruled by emotions than we are, because emotions come first, well before reason.

In order to predict, the brain builds an internal model of the world. In the course of action, the observed results are compared to the prediction, and the model is spontaneously modified, via plasticity, to predict better the next time around.

It is important to understand that this model is internally generated. Sensory input from the outside world modifies but doesn't fully define the model, which can function based on internal input (like it does in dreams or, say, in planning for the future), even in the absence of any sensory input from the outside. The brain is a virtual reality machine.

How, then, can we understand each other? Why aren't the internal models of different brains so different as to be mutually incomprehensible? Well, they are incomprehensible across different species. But within a species, the foundation of the model has the same evolutionary history. The model, after all, must adequately reflect the shared outside world for survival.

Via the action–feedback–action loop, the universals of the world are embedded, in the course of evolution, in the very structure of the brain. In [19], Llinás offers the metaphor of a gelatinous cube of electrically conductive material with electric contacts on its surface. The gelatin condenses into filaments if current passes often between the contacts but relaxes back to the amorphous state if no current flows for a while.

In this, you may already recognize the brain plasticity at work.

If the current is based on the sensory input from, for example, playing soccer, then eventually our cube of gelatin would develop a structure that, in a certain sense, *encodes* the rules of playing soccer, though it would be very different from the familiar game, with a ball, a team of players, and a referee.

Likewise, the brain encodes our experiences in a different format. It is meaningless to ask where exactly in the brain the images we see or our thoughts are to be found, for they are products of the entire process, encoded in our brain through *interaction* with the world—the action–feedback–action loop.

Though many degrees removed, our thinking is ultimately an internalization of our movement.

Leonid Korogodski

Galaxies in Plasma Lab

O NCE UPON A TIME, ASTRONOMERS THOUGHT THAT THE planets, the Sun, and the Moon all moved around the Earth in uniform circular motion. The heavens must be perfect, right? And what could be more perfect than a circle!

One problem: every now and then, planets reverse the direction of their visible motion across the sky, which would be impossible if they turned around the Earth on circular orbits. This so-called *retrograde motion* of planets forced the introduction of epicycles. An *epicycle* was a smaller circle on which a planet would turn around a certain point, which itself would turn on a circular orbit (a *deferent*) around the Earth.

If this sounds complex, you have seen nothing yet. Although retrograde motion now became possible, the calculations still didn't quite match the observations. Soon, epicycles on epicycles were invented, yet smaller circles on which the planets would turn around a certain point that would move along an epicycle that would move along a deferent around the Earth.

Where did all the original perfect simplicity go?

Unwilling to reconsider the basic assumption that the Earth was at the center, medieval astronomers kept shoring up the ailing geocentric system with *ad hoc* solutions.

This is a classic example of how science must not be done.

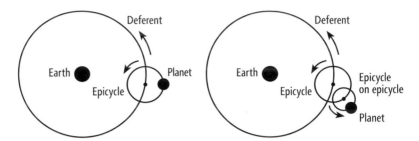

S OME TIME IN THE 1930S, ASTRONOMERS LEARNED HOW TO measure the velocities at which stars rotate around the centers of their galaxies, also known in the specialized scientific lingo as *rotation curves.* The results surprised them.

By the law of gravity, the stars closest to the center should rotate faster than those found farther away. This is how planets in the solar system rotate around the Sun. But the so-called rotation curves of galaxies were flat almost everywhere, meaning that the rotational velocities of stars around the center of the galaxy were just about equal, no matter what the distance from the center. The stars on the periphery were rotating way too fast. If the galaxy were held together only by the force of gravity, it should have long since fallen apart, ejecting the fast-rotating stars into the intergalactic space, like slingshots.

But this was the time when gravity was held in high esteem. For centuries since Newton, astronomy achieved many important results relying entirely on the law of gravity. And the General Relativity theory by Albert Einstein (1879–1955), only recently proposed and accepted, tickled scientists' minds and popular imagination. No one was about to suggest that anything but gravity ruled the universe at the galactic scale. Besides, there was no real alternative yet at that point in time.

Thus, *dark matter* was invented to shore up the gap discovered between theory and observation. No one was willing to suggest a new, unknown—or even an already known!—force other than gravity. But a new, unknown kind of matter that couldn't be made of any elementary particles known then (and even now), the kind of matter that neither absorbs nor emits

LEONID KOROGODSKI

electromagnetic radiation (like visible light, or radio, or infrared, etc.)—otherwise, it would have been detected by spectrography—and in general, doesn't affect the normal matter in any imaginable way but by exerting gravity? No problem! After all, the stars rotate so fast that there simply *must* be some additional mass lurking nearby.

Since then, dark matter was conveniently sprinkled anywhere it was needed to close yet another gap between theory and observation—and the number of such gaps kept mounting. New surprises, contradicting the generally accepted wisdom, were popping up like mushrooms almost anywhere one aimed a telescope. Naturally, the same kind of dark matter could not explain them all. So the variety kept growing. Soon we had cold dark matter, hot dark matter, warm dark matter, weakly interacting dark matter, strongly interacting dark matter, repulsive dark matter, self-annihilating dark matter, even fuzzy dark matter... none of which was ever observed, and not for the lack of trying. Moreover, the total amount of dark matter called upon dwarfed the visible matter many times over.

Somewhere along the way, scientists must have forgotten the venerable Occam's Razor principle: Do not invent new entities in vain!

The world hadn't seen the like of it since the infamous epicycles.

E NTER HANNES ALFVÉN (1908–1995). AN EXPERIMENTALIST with incredibly strong intuition, he would have felt himself at home in the 19th century, the time of hands-on experimental science and passionate inventors. Instead, he lived and worked during the era when theory dominated over experiment in certain fields, the era of an increasing compartmentalization of science and the rise of scientific bureaucracy. One of the pioneers of plasma physics, he crossed into the space sciences with new ideas, going against the established wisdom. Even after he received the Nobel Prize in Physics in 1970, he continued to be ignored by the astrophysical establishment.

Every single so-called "proof" of dark matter's existence to date is just like that: dark matter must exist because there would have been a gap between theory and observation otherwise. Duh!

Contrary to a common misconception, Occam's Razor principle does *not* say that a simpler explanation is more credible.

His sin was to maintain that the universe was made mostly not of dark matter but of plasma, a state of matter that contained charged particles (electrons and ions) instead of, or in addition to, neutral atoms—and consequently that the electromagnetic force played an equal or greater part than gravity at the galactic and supra-galactic scales.

Already in 1937, he predicted the existence of a galactic magnetic field. Before the space age, nothing seemed to portend such a discovery. Space was considered to be a vacuum, which obviously couldn't conduct electric currents, and so no magnetic field on such a scale was possible.

Of course, as soon as we went into space, we discovered that it was filled with plasma, electric currents, and magnetic fields. But even though the existence of electric currents in the solar system soon became common knowledge, galactic-scale electric currents continued to be denied.

The (in)famous Alfvén–Chapman controversy lasted for decades; it's symptomatic of the relationship between theory and experiment in the 20th century space sciences. The argument between Hannes Alfvén and Sydney Chapman (1888–1970) was about the nature of auroras. Chapman thought that the electric currents creating auroras existed entirely within the Earth's magnetosphere. Alfvén believed that there was an explicit Sun–Earth connection, continuing the tradition that began with Kristian Birkeland (1867–1917), a Norwegian scientist, inventor, and polar explorer, whose name Chapman had been systematically trying to erase from history of science.

Alfvén's is quoted in [9] on Chapman's approach to Birkeland's scientific legacy.

Chapman's theory was simple and mathematically elegant, while Alfvén's was the opposite. The matter couldn't be resolved before the space age, because the solution for the distribution of electric currents in space, based on the measurements on the surface of the Earth, was not unique; the measurements supported both models. But nearly as soon as we sent the first space probes, they literally flew into what's now called the *Birkeland filaments,* predicted by Birkeland and Alfvén.

So much for mathematical elegance.

LEONID KOROGODSKI

HANNES ALFVÉN PROPOSED THE PLASMA UNIVERSE PARA-digm, a radically new way of looking at the universe. It is based on two main principles:

- that the universe is made of plasma, for the most part; and
- that the fundamental properties of plasma are the same everywhere and at any scale.

The second one, the principle of scalability of plasma, is supported by direct measurements at the scales ranging from microscopic to the size of planetary systems. About the same number of degrees of magnitude separates the latter from superclusters of galaxies. It is not unreasonable to suppose that the principle of scalability of plasma holds at those scales as well. The Sloan Digital Sky Survey's discovery of a fractal structure (cf. [17]) suggests that this is indeed the case, for the fractal structure means self-similarity. The universe is made of filaments and cells ("great walls" of galaxies and empty voids), the structures typical of plasma's self-organization properties.

Perhaps the most fascinating thing about it is that astronomical events can be scaled down, in both space and time, to fit into a plasma lab. One can, for example, try to reproduce the formation and evolution of galaxies, however briefly!

THIS WAS DONE, SUCCESSFULLY, BY ANTHONY PERATT (B. 1940). His results were first published in 1986 in the IEEE Transactions on Plasma Science [25].

A graduate student of Alfvén, Peratt is now a member of the Associate Directorate of Los Alamos National Laboratory. At that time, he was working with Blackjack V at Maxwell Laboratories. Back then, this was the most powerful electromagnetic pulse generator, capable of producing briefly several times the power generating capacity of the entire human civilization. Ultra-fast photography of high-energy plasma discharges captured what seemed like mini-galaxies, complete with spirals, the same radiation patterns, and a suggestive evolution. Their rotation curves were flat.

IEEE: the Institute of Electrical and Electronics Engineers.

See also [30] for an account of experiments that reproduced the Martian blueberries in plasma discharges.

Intrigued, Peratt developed a theory and a computer model to also take gravity into account and simulate the real galaxies, one by one, always backing his results by direct experiments. His theory withstood all tests to date, without requiring modifications. Briefly, it can be summarized as follows.

U NLIKE GRAVITY THAT TENDS TO FORM ROUND BODIES, the electromagnetic force tends to form filaments, thanks to the so-called *electromagnetic pinch* that forces charged particles to do turns around the magnetic field lines in spirals as tight as possible.

Filaments of plasma parallel to both the electric and magnetic fields (called *Birkeland filaments*) play a crucial part in auroras and are common to the solar system. According to Peratt, the universe is filled with galactic-sized Birkeland filaments of very low density and current, producing so little radiation that they are very hard to detect.

Plasma is an excellent conductor, although not a perfect one. Thus, voltage can exist in plasma but primarily within narrow layers of charged particles, called double layers. Everywhere else, plasma is locally quasi-neutral, which means that the electrostatic force—the like charges repel, the unlike charges attract—can be ignored.

As plasma physics tells us, double layers form in narrow cross-sections along the filaments. This is where most of the voltage is squeezed into. More voltage means higher resistance. Therefore, matter accumulates within the double layers, where the galactic disks eventually form, like beads along a string.

Three major forces act on Birkeland filaments:

o The $1/r$ attractive electromagnetic force.

The electric current in each filament creates a magnetic field that exerts force on the other filament. Parallel electric currents of the same direction attract, while those of the opposite direction repel. In our case, this force is attractive and proportional to the product of current in the filaments.

LEONID KOROGODSKI

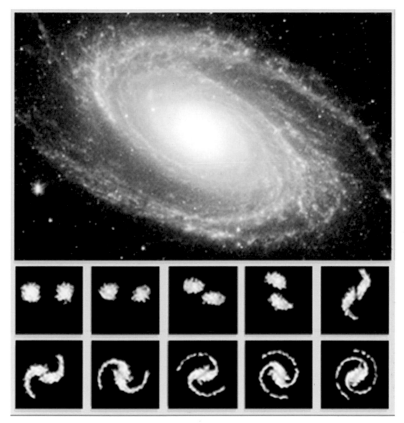

It depends on the distance r between them as $1/r$, if the filaments' lengths are much greater than r. This is because the current is the same along the entire length of each filament. This force is often called the Biot–Savart force.

o The $1/r^2$ force of gravity.

This force is proportional to the product of mass in the filaments. If plasma density were uniform along the filaments, this force would also have been $1/r$. But matter accumulates only in the relatively narrow cross-sections where double layers form. Elsewhere, mass is negligible, and therefore the force of gravity between the filaments is $1/r^2$.

○ The $1/r^4$ repulsive electromagnetic force.

Positively charged and negatively charged particles spiral around the magnetic field lines in opposite directions. This adds a circular (properly called *azimuthal*) component to the total electric current in the filaments. Azimuthal currents of the same orientation repel; of the opposite, attract. In our case, they repel. The cumulative force is proportional to the product of magnetic momenta of the filaments and behaves as $1/r^4$. Importantly, the interaction of these azimuthal currents also produces a torque that eventually makes the filaments turn around each other, like a hurricane.

Because it's $1/r$, the attractive electromagnetic force is dominant at the long range, but the $1/r^4$ repulsive force overtakes it at the close range. Simulations show that gravity does not make much impact at the galactic scale.

Because the attractive force is $1/r$, the plasma filaments usually form pairs, occasionally triples. The number of filaments determines the number of spiral arms to form. But one-armed galaxies are possible as well, if one of the filaments is too weak to produce stars.

Double radio galaxy is the first stage. The cross-sections of each filament emit the so-called *synchrotron radiation* in the radio range, a kind of electromagnetic radiation with a specific, recognizable spectrum, which can only be produced by relativistic electrons accelerating in an electric field.

QUASAR: a quasi-stellar radio source. Usually thought to be extremely far away, they may be actually much closer to us.

As the filaments are drawn toward each other, the plasma in the center is squeezed by the converging magnetic mirrors, producing a plasmoid that behaves like a quasar.

Eventually, the plasma in the center is compressed so much that stars begin to form in the elliptical sump, where the magnetic field is lower.

By this time, the short-range repulsive force is already felt, and the filaments begin to turn around each other, trailing plasma in the spiral arms, along which electric currents start to flow.

LEONID KOROGODSKI

A portion of the plasma filament connecting the galaxies NGC 1409 (right) and NGC 1410 (left) may have captured some dust and therefore turned visible. NASA/William C. Keel, University of Alabama.

The electromagnetic pinch in those currents compresses plasma such that, reaching a certain threshold, stars begin to form throughout the entire spiral arm at nearly the same time. This phenomenon is called *starburst*.

In fact, the condition for gravity to take over—and thus for round bodies, like stars, to form from filaments—is that the density divided by the electric current density must be greater than a certain constant. If the current is almost the same everywhere, this leads to the de Vaucouleurs relation that has been vexing our astronomers: for most of the stars in our galaxy, the mass divided by the radius is nearly the same.

This brief account doesn't go into many technical details and is far from rigorous. I must at this point refer the reader to the original article [25], as well as the monograph [26] and the popular science book [18].

PLASMA IS AN AMAZING STATE OF MATTER. IT DOES NOT behave like gas, especially when it's of low density (collisionless). The electromagnetic forces between moving particles make its behavior very complex, almost life-like. Plasma even got its name from a similarity with blood plasma, which coagulates around foreign bodies. Electromagnetic plasma forms double layers around solid bodies immersed in it, shielding them from electrostatic interaction (which is why it's very hard to determine if planets have significant non-zero electric charge). Double layers also form at the boundaries between plasmas with different physical characterstics (like temperature, chemical composition, etc.).

Plasma does not stay still. It writhes and bucks as if alive, behaving in ways difficult to predict by theory, as the fusion scientists have learned to their chagrin. Even Alfvén's intuition sometimes failed to anticipate plasma's behavior.

Formation of filaments and development of cellular structure are characteristic properties of plasma. At the large scale, the universe is made of "great walls" of galaxies separated by enormous voids. Within these walls, galaxies are strung along gigantic Birkeland filaments like beads on a string. So are stars within the galaxies.

During his controversy with Chapman, Alfvén fought against the tendency to consider the Earth as an isolated system. Not only is there the Sun–Earth plasma connection, but there also must be the Sun–Galaxy plasma connection, and so on to the ever larger scales.

In order to sustain complexity and to continue self-organization, a system must keep exchanging energy and entropy with its environment. Had the Sun been isolated from our Milky Way galaxy (except for the gravitational interaction), or had the Earth been likewise separated from the Sun, they would have long since succumbed to the "heat death" or, at the very least, would not have been able to keep the evolutionary spiral going. The galactic currents connected to the Sun's polar jets, the solar wind continuously engaged in complex interactions with the Earth's magnetosphere, the auroral currents influencing the atmospheric processes—all of this complexity may have allowed life to blossom on the Earth.

BIBLIOGRAPHY

THESE ARE SOME OF THE SOURCES THAT INFLUENCED THE story. With a few exceptions, scientific articles are not listed. For more information, please visit pinknoise.net.

[1] Alfvén, Hannes O.G. *Cosmic Plasma*. Springer–Verlag, 1981.

[2] Alfvén, Hannes O.G. *Cosmology in the Plasma Universe: An Introductory Exposition*. IEEE Transactions in Plasma Science, vol. 18, 1990.

[3] Barabási, Albert-Lázsló. *Linked: How Everything is Connected to Everything Else and What It Means*. Plume, 2003.

[4] Barthes, Roland. *Image–Music–Text*. Hill and Wang, 1978.

[5] Beinhocker, Eric D. *The Origin of Wealth: Evolution, Complexity, and the Radical Remaking of Economics*. Harvard Business School Press, 2006.

[6] Berglund, Axel-Ivar. *Zulu Thought-Patterns and Symbolism*. Indiana University Press, 1976.

[7] Buzsáki, György. *Rhythms of the Brain*. Oxford University Press, 2006.

[8] Carse, James P. *Finite and Infinite Games: A Vision of Life as Play and Possibility*. Ballantine Books, 1987.

[9] Christophorou, Loucas G. *Place of Science in a World of Values and Facts*. Innovations in Science Education and Technology. Springer, 2001.

[10] Dennett, Daniel C. *Consciousness Explained*. Back Bay Books, 1991.

[11] Edelman, Gerald M. *Neural Darwinism: The Theory of Neuronal Group Selection*. Basic Books, 1987.

[12] Edelman, Gerald M.; Guilio Tononi. *A Universe of Consciousness: How Matter Becomes Imagination*. Basic Books, 2000.

[13] Erlmann, Veit. *Nightsong: Performance, Power, and Practice in South Africa*. With an introduction by Joseph Shabalala. The University of Chicago Press, 1996.

[14] Gell-Mann, Murray. *The Quark and the Jaguar: Adventures in the Simple and the Complex*. Freeman & Co., 1994.

[15] Gregory, Lady Augusta; William B. Yeats. *Treasury of Irish Myth, Legend & Folklore: Fairy and Folk Tales of the Irish Peasantry*. Gramercy, 1988.

[16] Kalu, Ogbu U., ed. *African Christianity: An African Story*. Africa World Press, 2007.

[17] Khalil, Andre; Yongfeng Wu; David J. Batuski. *The Fractal Structure of the Universe: A Research from the Sloan Digital Sky Survey*. VDM Verlag, 2008.

[18] Lerner, Eric. *The Big Bang Never Happened*. Vintage, 1992.

[19] Llinás, Rodolfo R. *I of the Vortex: From Neurons to Self*. MIT Press, 2001.

[20] Lysaght, Patricia. *The Banshee: The Irish Death Messenger*. Robert Rinehart Publishers, 1986.

[21] McDermott, Rachel Fell; Jeffrey J. Kripal, eds. *Encountering Kali: In the Margins, at the Center, in the West*. University of California Press, 2003.

[22] Metzinger, Thomas. *Being No One: The Self-Model Theory of Subjectivity*. MIT Press, 2003.

[23] Moore, Thomas. *Dark Eros: The Imagination of Sadism*. Spring Publications, 1995.

[24] O'Shea, Janet. *At Home in the World: Bharata Natyam on the Global Stage*. Wesleyan University Press, 2007.

[25] Peratt, Anthony L. *Evolution of the Plasma Universe. Parts I and II*. IEEE Transactions in Plasma Science, vol. PS-14, no. 6, 1986.

[26] Peratt, Anthony L. *Physics of the Plasma Universe*. Springer-Verlag, 1992.

[27] Peratt, Anthony L. *Characteristics for the Occurrence of a High-Current, z-Pinch Aurora as Recorded in Antiquity*. IEEE Transactions in Plasma Science, vol. 31, no. 6, 2003.

[28] Pope, G.U.; W.H. Drew; John Lazarus; F.W. Ellis, trs. *Tirukkural: English Translation and Commentary*. W.H. Allen & Co., 1886.

[29] Prigogine, Ilya R. *The End of Certainty*. Free Press, 1997.

[30] Ransom, C.J.; W. Thornhill. *Plasma-Generated Craters and Spherules*. IEEE Transactions on Plasma Science, 35:4, 2007.

[31] Scott, Donald E. *The Electric Sky*. Mikamar Publishing, 2006.

[32] Strogatz, Steven H. *Sync: How Order Emerges from Chaos in the Universe, Nature, and Daily Life*. Hyperion, 2003.

[33] Sunkdler, Bengt G.M. *Bantu Prophets in South Africa*. James Clarke Lutterworth, 2004.

[34] Wolfram, Stephen. *A New Kind of Science*. Wolfram Media, 2002.

[35] Zarrilli, Phillip B. *When the Body Becomes All Eyes: Paradigms, Discourses and Practices of Power in Kalarippayattu, a South Indian Martial Art*. Oxford University Press, 1998.

APPENDICES

THE NOSE BRIDGE, HELLAS PLANITIA, MARS

GLOSSARY

abakhaya [ZULU]
"Home people," from *ikhaya,* "home." A close community of friends and neighbors.

abathakathi [ZULU]
The plural form of *umthakathi.*

African Christianity
African Instituted, or Independent, Churches (AIC) is one of the major branches of Christianity, different from Catholic, Protestant, Orthodox, and Pentecostal branches. It used to be called syncretist for borrowing some elements of native cultures. But it is no more than what early Christianity had borrowed from the Greeks.
See also *Zulu Zionists.*

Alfvén limiting current
The upper limit on the strength of electric current in vacuum in the absence of a background magnetic field.

Alfvén waves
A kind of magnetohydrodynamic wave in plasma. While gas has only one wave mode (that is, sound), plasma has many, including also magnetosonic waves, whistler waves, Langmuir waves, and many others. Alfvén waves are transverse waves of magnetic field and ion density, propagating parallel to the magnetic field.

alpha-helix
One of the two main geometric motifs in the structure of protein molecules, alpha-helix resembles a coiled spring.
See also *beta-sheet.*

amadlozi [Zulu]

The plural form of *idlozi.*

amaZiyoni [Zulu]

The plural form of *iZiyoni,* a Zionist.

amnesia

Loss of existing memories is called *posterograde* amnesia. Damage to the hippocampus often leads to *anterograde* amnesia, the inability to form or retain new memories.

analog, *adj.*

Characterized by continuity of state, as opposed to *digital,* which is distinguished by having discrete states.

ankam [Malayalam: അങ്കം]

Duel to the death in the medieval Kerala, as a method of settling disputes. The fighters normally were members of the Chekavar caste, representing their high-caste patrons.

See also *Chekavar.*

anterior cingulate cortex

The cingulate cortex is a collar-shaped part of the brain wrapped around the corpus callosum that connects the hemispheres. Its frontal part is called anterior.

artificial, *aka* **artie**

Sentient cyber-being created from scratch, as opposed to having had their minds transferred into the digital format, as the posthuman minds are. Note that this term does not apply to the Wish Fairies, whose origin remains unknown. Referred to by the *sie* (her, hers) pronoun.

astrocyte

A star-shaped glial cell, found in the brain and in the spinal cord.

See also *glial cells.*

ATP

Adenosine triphosphate. This small molecule is the sole bottomline source of energy for all known life forms. Produced by *ATP synthase.*

ATP synthase

An enzyme that produces ATP, the cell's "energy currency." The molecule consists of F_0—a part embedded in the mitochondrial membrane; F_1—a part sticking out; and an axle threaded through both.

An electric gradient across the membrane is generated by a complex cycle of chemical reactions involving either oxygen or photosynthesis (or certain other means, like in chemolithotropes). This makes protons (H^+) flow across the membrane, using F_0 as a tunnel.

This electric current turns the axle. As it rotates inside the stalk, its catalytic sites go through a series of changes, making ATP.

aurora

On Earth, also known as the northern polar lights (aurora borealis) and the southern polar lights (aurora australis). But on Mars, it's not confined to the polar regions and is mainly ultraviolet.

basal ganglia

A group of brain nuclei located near the center of the brain, the basal ganglia is a repository of faps, fixed action patterns. Damage to the basal ganglia, in particular to its part called *substantia nigra,* is involved in Parkinson's disease.

bean sidhe [IRISH]

Translated literally, "fairy woman." *Banshee* in English.

Bean sidhe is a female spirit, a supernatural death messenger. Despite the mutation of banshee into an evil monster that supposedly kills with its cry, the authentic Irish *bean sidhe* is a benevolent spirit, following some families as guardians. When someone in the family is soon to die, she appears as a beautiful woman in white and cries mournfully.

Another manifestation of *bean sidhe,* called *badhb* (pronounced like "bibe"), is a hideous hag washing severed heads and limbs as a sign of impending death, just like the Scottish *bean nighe,* the Washer-at-the-Ford.

See also *decapitation game.*

In Ireland, *bean sidhe* is sometimes said to cry a person, instead of crying *for* a person.

beta-sheet

One of the main geometric motifs in the structure of protein molecules. The pattern consists of wavy strands extending side by side.

See also *alpha-helix.*

bleed

In drawing, when a part of an object is cut off by an edge of the drawing area, it is said that the object is bleeding. The same terminology is also used in painting, printing, and photography.

blind drawing

A method of drawing where the artist does not look at the drawing itself. The hand with the drawing tool moves without being observed by eyes. The artist may look at the model, but the eyes must not see the drawing-in-progress.

blind spot

A special zone in the field of vision of a *blindsight* patient.

Blindsight is a neurological condition when one cannot consciously perceive objects in a certain part of one's field of vision. However, if one throws, say, a ball at the patient, hidden entirely within the blind spot, still the patient may—and often does—unconsciously react and catch it.

The eyes do see, and the brain processes the signals, but the patient doesn't have a *conscious* access to that information.

blueberries, Martian

Small blueish-gray spherules found peppering the surface in many locations on Mars. Most are about the size of a pea, of various shapes, from round balls to hollow cylinders, but most of them have an axis of rotation. The closest Earth analog is the Moqui balls in Utah.

butterfly wing

A kind of mast on magsail ships of the frigate class.

See also *magnetic sail.*

checksum

In computing and communications, a number or other kind of data generated from a larger body of data such that if the original data is tampered with, the checksum computed once again would differ from the original checksum. Thus, one can detect intrusion and try to recover the unspoiled data, if possible.

Chekavar [Mᴀʟᴀʏᴀʟᴀᴍ: ചേക്കവർ]

A subcaste of the Ellava, aka Thiyya, a human caste in Kerala, South India. Chekavar men were brought up to fight in the *ankam,* duels to the death, as champions of the disputing parties that were members of higher castes. Chekavar fighters practiced the South Indian martial art of *kalaripayyatt,* the art of vital points.

See also *ankam* and *kalarippayatt.*

choreoathetosis

Sydenham's chorea is also known as St. Vitus' Dance.

A combination of *chorea* and *athetosis.* Chorea is a neurological condition characterized by involuntary, irregular muscle contractions that are not rhythmic but appear to flow from one muscle to the next. The movements caused by these contractions have a dance-like quality, which is why they were called "chorea"—from "choreography." Athetosis also adds involuntary jerky, writhing movements.

collagen

The main protein component of the connective tissue in animals. Fibers of collagen are very strong, which is why it is found in skin, bone, ligaments, tendons, and other places where a good tensile

strength is necessary. Together with keratin, it gives skin its strength and elasticity. Degradation of collagen is the cause of age wrinkles.
See also *keratin.*

conjunction, planetary

An astronomical event when two or more planets are arranged along the same line with the Sun. For any pair of planets from the set, the conjunction is called inferior if the planets are on the same side from the Sun along that line, and superior if they are opposite.

coulage

A technique in surrealistic art where a sculpture is produced by pouring molten wax—or other suitable material, like chocolate—into cold water. Not to be confused with *collage.*

Cryptic Region

One of the most beautiful places on Mars. This large area near the south pole was called Cryptic for it mysteriously darkens early in the southern spring, while the rest of the polar cap stays bright, still covered with ice (see the albedo—brightness—map on page 6).

The darkening is caused by the so-called "dalmatian spots," dark splotches with fan-like extensions. These are made by jets of dark material shooting from beneath the ice as soon as it begins to melt—possibly, a mix of frozen carbon dioxide and petroleum.

Some of the ice is melted by the Sun, when it appears after the long polar night. But some is melted by the energetic solar particles that, passing through thin atmosphere, strike the ice in curtains of magnetic field-aligned electric current filaments, leaving characteristic patterns in the ice.

Thanks to its eccentric—that is, elongated—orbit in the Sun's radial electric field, Mars passes through areas of rapidly changing potential in the southern spring, so the process intensifies. Its high eccentricity makes Mars susceptible to electromagnetic weathering.

ADVANCED: Abiogenic petroleum could have formed by the Plausson process, driven by the relativistic Weibel instability.

dalmatian spots, on Mars

See *Cryptic Region.*

decapitation game

A common theme in ancient Celtic myths. A mysterious man offers three famous Irish heroes a game: they would cut off his head tonight, under the condition that the next day their roles are reversed.

The first two heroes decide to play, but their courage fails by the next day, after they see the beheaded man miraculously pick up his head from the floor and leave. Finally, Cú Chulainn plays. He waits

The same motif is found in *Sir Gawain and the Green Knight,* an Arthurian tale.

D

for the man to come back, then puts his head on the block. But he is spared. The mysterious man turns out to be a druid who came to test the heroes' courage.

decorticate rigidity

Involuntary flexion or extension of muscles by person in a coma indicates brain damage in the cortex and/or that the interface between the cortex and the rest of the motor system is affected.

The arms are bent at the elbows up and toward each other, connecting over the chest. The fists are clenched and pressed against each other. The legs are extended, with feet turned inward.

diamond nanorods

A super-hard material, not only harder than diamond but even harder than *fullerite,* a macroscopic form of *buckyballs,* the carbon-cage molecules like C_{60}. Diamond nanorods are made by crushing buckyballs under tremendous pressure. Also known as *hyperdiamond.*

digital, *adj.*

Characterized by discreteness of states, as opposed to *analog.*

Doppler shift

The change of wavelength observed when either the source of the waves or the medium in which they propagate moves relative to the observer. For visible light, wavelength corresponds to color. So it is common to call lowering of frequency the "red shift," and the opposite of it the "blue shift."

double layer

Plasma envelops any object with two parallel layers of oppositely charged particles, with a very thin space in between, such that the object is shielded from electrostatic interaction with the outside. Because of this resemblance with blood plasma that coagulates around any foreign body, Irving Langmuir (1881–1957), the 1932 Nobel Laureate in Chemistry, called this state of matter *plasma.*

Double layers form at the boundary between plasma regions with different characteristics (temperature, density, chemical composition, and so on). Charge separation does exist in plasma—but most of the voltage is squeezed into layers as narrow as possible.

Drakensberg

A mountain range in KwaZulu–Natal, South Africa, running parallel to the southeastern coast for about 1,000 km. Its highest elevation is just below 3.5 km above the sea level. In Zulu, it's called *uKhahlamba,* "Barrier of Spears."

For many centuries, the mountains were inhabited by the San (aka Bushmen), who left between 35,000 and 40,000 paintings on the walls of the numerous caves—the largest and most concentrated collection of cave art in the world.

See also *San*.

Dungeon Heart

In the *Dungeon Keeper* series of games, this is a giant heart beating within the inner sanctum of the dungeon, containing the player's life force. Once it is destroyed, the game is lost.

See also *Dungeon Keeper*.

Dungeon Keeper

A computer game developed by Peter Molyneux (b. 1959). Released in 1997, it was followed by a sequel, *Dungeon Keeper 2*, in 1999.

In the game, one plays an anti-hero, the evil keeper of a dungeon. The player builds a dungeon and makes improvements to it, populates it with evil minions, and defends it from intruders—the forces of Good and rival keepers alike—and may invade the territory of the enemy and have it, in the game terms, "claimed."

dust devil

On Earth, a dust devil is a small tornado. On Mars, dust devils are extremely common and can reach great heights, rising taller than Olympus Mons. On Earth, the dust devil is a solitary critter, but Martian dust devils often travel in packs and can even form an uninterrupted front.

On Mars, the field lines of the interplanetary magnetic field often pass straight through the surface. Dust devils are electrically charged dust rotating around the magnetic field lines. Vast quantities of electrified dust remain hanging in the atmosphere for days after dust storms, suspended in the double layers.

On Earth, dust devils produce radio noise and electrostatic fields of more than 10,000 volts per meter. On Mars, their bases *glow*.

Lunar dust, also, often hangs above the ground—even without *any* atmosphere.

dysrhythmia

Arises when gamma oscillations in the thalamocortical system are adversely affected by a resonance with lower frequency brainwaves, the so-called *edge effect*. It is an important part of the neurological basis for many psychological disorders. Discovered by Rodolfo Llinás.

electromagnetic pinch

Also known as z-pinch and Bennett pinch, this is the force that compresses plasma into filaments in a magnetic field.

E

Positively charged particles spiral around the magnetic field lines clockwise, when looking in the magnetic field's direction, and negatively charged ones spiral counterclockwise. The Lorentz force is directed toward the axis of rotation. In other words, the magnetic field "wants" the particle to make a tighter spiral.

This is what makes lightning so pinched and forky-looking.

E

electromagnetic pulse, *aka* **EMP**

An explosive, high-intensity and short-duration burst of electromagnetic radiation. The rapidly fluctuating magnetic field, if strong enough, can fry unprotected electronic equipment.

See also *Faraday cage.*

ELF waves

Extremely Low Frequency waves are under 30 Hz in frequency. They are used for communication with submarines because the higher frequencies can't penetrate sea water. But ELF communication is mind-numbingly slow, at the whooping rate of up to 30 *bits* a second.

exception

Special conditions arising in computing systems. Exceptions can be "caught" and processed to respond to the condition.

falcon mast

A kind of mast on magsail ships.

See also *magnetic sail.*

Faraday cage

An enclosure made of a conducting material, often in the form of a fine mesh, the Faraday cage protects any electronic equipment placed inside it against an external static electric field (or an external variable magnetic field, which amounts to the same thing), because electric charges inside the conducting material of the cage are automatically redistributed over the surface in response to the external field, neutralizing it inside the cage.

The thicker the walls of the cage and the smaller the openings in its lattice, the more powerful must the pulse be to break through.

See also *electromagnetic pulse.*

ferrofluid

A liquid of nanoparticles suspended in a carrier fluid such that its properties are affected by magnetic field. Ferrofluids that solidify in the presence of magnetic field are used in *Pink Noise* to make lightweight emergency armor.

See also *magnetorheological material.*

flywheel

   Quite simply, a wheel used for energy storage as it keeps spinning, and spinning, and—you guessed it—spinning. The faster it spins, the more energy it stores in the form of rotational energy.

   See also *power needle*.

foliation

   A mathematical concept. Informally speaking, a foliation is a division of a higher-dimensional body (properly called a "manifold") into a set of "slices" of a lower dimension. Think of an egg sliced very thin, though the slices don't have to be flat like planes.

G

gamma oscillations

   The historical name for brainwaves in the 30–80 hertz frequency range. The 40–50 hertz waves in the thalamocortical system are closely linked with consciousness.

geno-song

   Julia Kristeva (b. 1941) introduced the concepts of *geno-text* and *pheno-text* into the then-new discipline of semiology, the study of cultural signs. Roland Barthes (1915–1980) extended them to music.

   Pheno-song is all about meaning, not only through words but also through melody, rhythm, and by other means. *Geno-song,* on the other hand, is the "grain" of the song, the ineffable quality that gives it a character, a personality—"the body in the voice as it sings." [4]

Gilles de Rais (1404–1440)

   Gilles de Montmorency-Laval, Baron of Rais, Count of Brienne, Marshal of France, nicknamed Bluebeard, was a companion of Joan of Arc and the most notorious serial killer and pedophile of the Middle Ages. Executed in 1440 for sodomy, murder, and witchcraft, by hanging (which was rare for a nobleman).

   The number of his victims is variously estimated from 80 to 600, ranging in age from six to eighteen, of both sexes. Gilles de Rais was especially fond of torturing and killing boys with blond hair and blue eyes, resembling himself.

glial cells

   Also known as *glia,* these are certain kinds of cells in the brain that provide support to neurons.

   See also *astrocyte*.

Great Red Spot

   An enormous plasma vortex on Jupiter, the Great Red Spot is an elongated oval at about 22° South, with slight but regular oscillations of its latitude. Its dimensions have varied widely over the centuries, from 40,000×14,000 km down to 10,000×3,000 km (the Earth's diameter is 12,740 km), depending sensitively on the solar activity.

The Great Red Spot owes its name to the brick-red color that it possesses most often, although its color can change rapidly, on occasion totally disappearing from the visible range; when that happens, it looks like an enormous hole in the planet—or a sunspot.

H

hachure

An artistic technique where thinly spaced, short parallel lines are used in drawing to create the impression of a three-dimensional shape. The word *hachure* is French for "hatching," another name for the technique. *Cross-hatching* uses similar lines crossing at an angle.

Hamiltonian potential

For a vector field, a Hamiltonian potential is a function whose value is constant along the field lines. In classical mechanics, it stands for the system's energy. Its constancy is the energy conservation law. In quantum mechanics, the Hamiltonian is defined differently, as an operator. But it means the same—the system's energy.

Hand of Evil

In the *Dungeon Keeper* series of games, the Hand of Evil is the cursor. One can use it to slap one's minions, making them work harder, or on prisoners in torture chambers.

See also *Dungeon Keeper*.

Hellas Planitia

A huge depression in the southern hemisphere of Mars. Hellas Planitia is about 2,300 km wide, nearly the same as the length of the entire Himalaya chain of mountains on Earth. Hellas is 9 km deep, from rim to bottom, enough to cover the top of Everest. The rim is made of a circular chain of mountains, about 2 km tall. Hellas is home to some of the most exotic terrain in the solar system.

hemineglect

A neurological condition caused by damage to certain parts of one hemisphere of the brain that makes it difficult or impossible for the patient to perceive the corresponding half of the perception field. In some cases, the patient doesn't perceive anything on one side of their entire field of vision. In others, the patient can see only one side of every object.

The amazing thing about hemineglect is that it doesn't feel as if anything is missing from the world. No matter what happens,

The author is a fan of the "singular they."

consciousness always "closes" around the gaps, presenting an unbroken new model of the world, with the overwhelming sense of it being complete.

hippocampus

The brain's search engine, the hippocampus works by bridging space and time. The so-called *place cells* in the hippocampus form a "map" of sorts, firing in the fashion that is dependent on the body's current location. As we move, it's like a solitary wave centered on its location moving across the "place map."

The same place cells are responsible for navigating our memories. The *episodic* memories are linearly organized, along the arrow of time. But the *semantic* memory—of concepts rather than events—is based on "place maps" rather than paths. Building a map requires making trips down intersecting paths. In the same way, seeing one dog then another dog and so on eventually gives us the abstract idea of a "dog" in general. The concepts are like two-dimensional maps built from the intersecting paths of episodic memory.

honeycomb terrain

A rare kind of terrain found on Mars, in the deepest part of Hellas Planitia. The roughly oval and hexagonal depressions are separated by raised-lip walls with leaf-like patterns. The floor is often drawn with alternating light and dark bands.

idlozi, *pl.* amadlozi [Zulu]

Ancestor shade. In the traditionalist Zulu worldview, the deceased continue to exist in a very real sense. They stay in touch with their survivors via *izangoma,* to whom they appear in dreams and visions. In this context, they are also called *amathongo,* from *ubuthongo,* "sleep"—literally, "dream beings."

Amadlozi aren't worshipped but venerated as elder members of the lineage that now happen to be closer to *iNkosi yeZulu,* the Lord-of-Heaven, who alone can be worshipped. But direct prayers to the Lord-of-Heaven are rare. Believers usually ask their ancestor shades to intercede on their behalf.

See also *isangoma.*

iminqwamba [Zulu]

When a novice begins training to become an *isangoma,* a strip of skin, cut from the back of a sacrificial goat, is tied over the novice's left shoulder in a loop under the right arm. This skin is called *inqwamba* (in plural, *iminqwamba*).

At the completion of training, a second skin is tied over the novice's right shoulder in a loop under the left arm, the two *iminqwamba* forming a cross over the chest and at the back. This is a sign that the novice has completed training and is now a full *isangoma*.

See also *isangoma*.

indiki, *pl.* **amandiki** [Zulu]

A male *idlozi* (ancestor shade) that has developed a close personal relationship, to the point of possession, with an *isangoma*. The corresponding female idlozi is called *indawe*.

See also *idlozi* and *isangoma*.

ingoma ebusuku [Zulu]

See *isicathamiya*.

interneuron

At first, any neuron placed between its sensory and motor cousins in a signal chain was called an *interneuron*. But this defined most of the neurons in the brain. Now only the inhibitory neurons in the brain are called this.

Io–Jupiter electrical discharge

In 1979, flying by Jupiter's moon Io, the space probe Voyager 1 discovered what appeared to be volcanic plumes... except that they did not behave like ones. They were extraordinarily long, reaching nearly 300 km into space. They displayed prominent filamentary structure. And they *walked* across the surface, too!

In truth, the plumes of Io likely are intense electric currents of sustained megaamperes that excavate material and jet it into space, like EDM (electrical discharge machining) on steroids. Similar discharges are observed on other major satellites, although not as strong.

ion channel

A complex biomolecule embedded in the cellular membrane that can selectively let certain kinds of ions through. Some are *voltage-gated,* meaning that they open when the voltage across the membrane reaches a certain threshold. Some are *ligand-gated,* requiring the action of certain chemicals. Some use both mechanisms.

Neurons are especially rich in ion channels. Every one of them is like a stupendously complex computer chip, with ion channels acting like semiconductor gates.

isangoma, *pl.* **izangoma** [Zulu]

Isangoma is a conduit between ancestor shades, the *amadlozi,* and the living. Contact with the *amadlozi* can occur in the normal, everyday world while the *isangoma* is awake. But more often, this happens in dreams.

The occupation of *isangoma* is not hereditary. Few actually look forward to it. One is chosen by the *amadlozi,* which may happen suddenly at any age. This is usually signaled by extraordinary dreams and visions, a characteristic pain in the shoulders, neck, and side muscles, and/or upper back, and other symptoms. Mentally, the chosen is troubled, restless. It is said that the shades "brood"—*ukufuma*—over people, sitting on their minds like hens on eggs.

Acceptance, the subsequent training, and the rigors and restrictions of the life of *isangoma* do not so much *heal* her (less often, him) as *channel* her affliction into another course, transforming it into something positive. *Izangoma* are good at treating mental illnesses. Many treat physical maladies as well.

Catching the *abathakathi,* the purported evil sorcerers and witches, is another important function of the *izangoma.*

isicathamiya [Zulu]

A uniquely Zulu musical genre, *isicathamiya* is a combination of male *a cappella* singing with a peculiar dancing style.

The name comes from the root -*cathama,* "walk like a cat." In contrast to the vigorous foot thumping of the war-like dancing of the 19th century, *isicathamiya* singer-dancers literally dance on their tiptoes.

Singing in *isicathamiya* is based on four-part harmony but with many Zulu elements. Polyphony tends to converge like horns of buffalo. There is usually one high soprano voice, and many basses.

ixhanthi [Zulu]

The "snake of diviners," a fabuous animal that can only be perceived by the *izangoma.* In the common language, the word *ixhanthi* means the upper row of dorsal vertebrae. Not so to the *izangoma.*

izangoma [Zulu]

The plural form of *isangoma.*

kalarippayatt [Malayalam: കളരിപയറ്റ്]

An ancient South Indian martial art, *kalarippayatt* (aka *kalarippayattu*) is the oldest martial art in the world, rooted in the poetic, martial culture of the Dravidian South India.

Kalari, in both Tamil and Malayalam, means the combat pit. *Payatt* is practice, in the latter. In Tamil, the same martial art is also known as *varma kalari* or *varma ati*—the art of vital points. *Varmam* in Tamil—*marmam* in Malayalam—are special points in one's physical and "subtle" bodies that regulate the flow of cosmic energy, *prana.* When such a point is harmed, the victim can become severely ill, disabled, or can even die—immediately or by slow decay. The same points can be used to heal.

See also *Chekavar, Kali, Kerala,* and *Unniyarcha.*

Kali

K

There are also many Christian and Muslim *kalari.*

The Hindu goddess of war and death, Kali is perhaps the only non-vegetarian in the pantheon, requiring blood sacrifice of animals. She is likely to be of a Dravidian origin, at least to a great extent, although traits of several deities, both Dravidian and Arian alike, must have merged in Kali.

In her furious manifestation, Bhadrakali, she has always been venerated by the martial-minded people, especially in South India. Every Hindu *kalari,* a place for practicing the martial art of *kalarip-payatt,* has an idol of Bhadrakali. She is also popular in Bengal, where her "mother goddess" quality is emphasized, although clearly both aspects of the deity are found, to a varying extent, throughout India. The famous Bengali poet Ramprasad Sen (1720–1781) devoted most of his work to Kali.

In the 19th century, the followers of Kali were accused by the British of the so-called Thuggee (the origin of the English word "thug"), a supposed cult practice of killing innocent travelers and using them as human sacrifices. The idea was concocted in 1830 by then Captain W. Henry "Thuggee" Sleeman and provided an excellent pretext for the British to crack down on the warlike groups in India.

Kerala

A state in South India, Kerala occupies a strip of land between the Malabar coast in the west and the mountains separating it from Tamil Nadu in the east. Its native language is Malayalam, a member of the Dravidian family and a close relative of Tamil. The Malayalee culture is one of the offshots of the ancient Tamil culture.

Throughout much of its history, Kerala was the site of the ancient Chera kingdom and then of the medieval Chera kingdom. It was many times invaded by the Tamil. The struggle to maintain independence from the powerful Chola empire to the east lasted many centuries, fostering strong martial traditions.

Kerala is home to a large and thriving Christian community with ancient roots. It was established in the 1st century AD by Saint Thomas, the apostle sent to convert India. The first Portuguese travelers in the 16th century were surprised to discover strong Christian churches that were totally unlike any brand of Christianity they knew. Kerala's Jewish community goes even further back in history, to the establishment of a permanent Hebrew trade colony during the reign of King Solomon— including members of *all* tribes.

    See also *Chekavar* and *kalarippayatt.*

keratin
A very strong, tough protein that makes nails and hair in humans, as well as claws and all sorts of carapaces in other animals, so hard to break. Also found in skin, where it complements the elastic collagen.

    See also *collagen.*

kwaito
A popular genre of electronic music in South Africa, *kwaito* is influenced by European house music and African rhythms and melodies.

    It got its name from the Isicamtho word for "cool." Isicamtho is a new language with roots in the gangster subculture that developed from an amalgam of many African languages spoken in South Africa, as well as English and Afrikaans; the grammatical matrix is mainly Zulu and Sotho. Though not officially recognized, Isicamtho is the first language of many young South Africans.

    Kwaito became especially prominent during the post-apartheid era, when it became the principal medium of musical self-expression of the young generation. It's very rhythmic, often rough, and always danceable. There are many good *kwaito* bands, but the author's personal favorite is *Bongo Maffin.*

Langmuir waves
A kind of electrostatic wave in plasma, Langmuir wave is a periodic oscillation of electric charge. They can be produced by lasers pushing the electrons on their way through plasma. Langmuir waves are very fast, traveling almost at the speed of light, and can accelerate charged particles that follow in phase with the wave.

laser nanocavity
An important element in photonic networks.

    See also *photonic network.*

layered terrain
A picturesque terrain found in many places on Mars, but primarily in the polar regions where hills are finely terraced over enormous areas. Likely a product of electromagnetic weathering.

    See also *Cryptic Region.*

L

left hand side wife

Not what you may think!—*that* is up to each individual family.

The Zulu allow polygamy, even in the Zulu Zionist Christian denominations. In a traditional village, the hut of the first wife is to the right of the main hut; the hut of the second wife is to the left. The third wife is subordinate to the first wife and lives in the next hut on the right. Likewise, the fourth wife is subordinate to the second wife and lives in the next hut on the left. And so on.

Lichtenberg figure

Also known as "electric trees," Lichtenberg figures are finely branching shapes that form on the surface or in the interior of non-conducting materials as a product of dielectric breakdown in the process called *electric treeing.*

See also *Martian spider.*

lightning flower

See *Lichtenberg figure.*

long memory effect

Dependence of a system's behavior not only on the current state but also on its history, on the particular path taken to arrive at the current state. Long memory effect is a characteristic feature of complex adaptive systems.

Lough-an-Leagh

A lake by its namesake mountain in Ireland, Lough-an-Leagh is the "Lake of Healing" in Irish folklore. Its dark mud reputedly has many healing properties.

lucid dream

A state of consciousness experienced during sleep. It differs from ordinary dream in that the person is aware he or she is dreaming.

magnetic field of Mars

Although today Mars has no planetary magnetic field, there are many local magnetic anomalies, possibly the remains of the ancient planetary magnetic field. Most are found in the southern hemisphere. The strongest anomalies stretch in latitudinal bands across the 180° meridian, the southernmost not far from the south polar region.

magnetic sail

A long, closed loop of superconducting wire, also known as *magsail.* The magnetic field generated by the electric current in the loop deflects the solar wind's charged particles, creating a propulsive force in the opposite direction.

Magnetic sails are radically different from—and vastly superior to—solar sails, which are pushed by radiation pressure. Magsails slide sideways, except in one configuration when a magsail is strictly perpendicular to the solar wind (but this is difficult to maintain and untypical of magsail navigation). Unlike solar sails, magnetic sails provide an unprecedented degree of maneuverability.

See also *right-hand rule.*

magnetopause

The narrow boundary between the solar wind and a planetary magnetosphere (or plasmasphere, in the absence of magnetic field). A double layer always forms in the magnetopause.

See also *double layer* and *solar wind.*

magnetorheological material

Similar to ferrofluid, this is a fluid that hardens in the presence of magnetic field. But while ferrofluid is made of nanoparticles, magnetorheological materials are coarser, with the particle sizes measured in microns.

See also *ferrofluid.*

magnetotail

See *plasmatail.*

mana

A staple of wizard-and-sorcery games, mana is a quantity necessary to cast spells. A spell typically requires the player to spend a certain amount of mana, which is replenished with time.

Martian spider

A peculiar fixture of the Martian terrain in the south polar region, Martian spiders are radially branching networks of channels in the surface, in some ways similar to Lichtenberg figures produced by the process called *electric treeing.* Also known as Arthur Clarke's trees.

See also *Cryptic Region* and *Lichtenberg figure.*

Mentor

In the *Dungeon Keeper* series of games, the Mentor is a cyber-assistant to the keeper. His advice can be very helpful when learning the ropes. And he has a certain sense of humor. The same cannot be said about the Gilles' Mentor in the story.

See also *Dungeon Keeper.*

metamaterial

A material whose properties depend not so much on what it's made of but on its internal artificially engineered structure. Metamaterials

can exhibit properties not readily found in nature. Thus, the so-called *left-handed metamaterials* refract light in the "wrong" way, as shown by the diagram on page 68. Metamaterials are also used in photonic networks, "invisibility cloaks," and other applications.
See also *laser nanocavity, polaritonic cloak,* and *superlens.*

mini-magnetospheric anti-plasma shield

M

A strong magnetic field that deflects charged particles away from the protected area.

mitochondria

An important part of the biological cell's structure. It is in the mito-chondria that ATP, the energy currency of life, is produced.

multiple redundancy

The principle of having numerous backups on standby to replace a failing unit.

mudra

A symbolic gesture in Hinduism and Buddhism, often as part of a ritual. In *Pink Noise,* the word is used in a more specific way—the stylized hand gestures in *bharatanatyam,* a classical dance of India. From these expressive gestures, also known as *hastas,* an intuitive vocabulary for the Dragon Guard's fighting dance with Dragonclaws was developed, reducing the calculation load for coordinating the movement of the laser beams.

nanotorus, *pl.* **nanotori**

A nanoparticle in the shape of a torus. Nanotori are famous for their predicted ability to store a substantial magnetic moment. None have been produced yet, to the best of the author's knowledge.

Nguni

The common ancestors of Zulu and Xhosa, who migrated into Southern Africa around the 4th century AD.

nhliziyo [Zulu]

Usually translated as "heart," this word actually stands for an area of the throat that traditionally is considered the seat of emotions in the Zulu culture, as the heart is in the West.

Occam's Razor

ENTIA NON SUNT MULTIPLICANDA PRAETER NECESSITATEM.
Entities must not be multiplied beyond necessity.—William of Ockham.
Formulated by William of Ockham (c. 1288–c. 1348), this philo-sophic principle is often incorrectly paraphrased as "when two theo-ries make the same predictions, the simpler one is to be preferred."

Explaining UFOs as alien spaceships is very simple but doesn't make this "theory" a better choice.

osmosis, osmotic
Osmosis is the diffusion of water through a semi-permeable membrane, with a preferred direction.

overclocking
Increasing the processing power of a computing system by increasing the frequency of its oscillations. In modern computers, this is usually applied to the CPU and GPU frequencies. Although the brain has no master clock, some brainwaves can be accelerated pharmaceutically for brief periods of time.

P

parahuman
A human whose brain is augmented with a digital component. Although the established term "cyborg" is applicable, it feels dehumanizing, as if the cyber is *instead* of the human and not *in addition* to it. The author wished to place the emphasis on the human.

paramagnetic
If a material only becomes a magnet in the presence of an external magnetic field, it is called *paramagnetic.*

parsec
A unit of length in astronomy equal to about 30.857 trillion kilometers (approximately, 19 trillion miles), or 3.26 light years.

peacock tail
A kind of mast on magsail ships of almost any class.
See also *magnetic sail.*

phase transition
A change in the state of matter; for example, from liquid to solid or gas.

photonic network
A network in which signals are passed not by electric current in conducting wires but by photons (light) in waveguides. Photonic crystals, a kind of metamaterial, are used to control the motion of photons.
See also *metamaterial* and *waveguide.*

place cells
See *hippocampus.*

plasmatail
The part of a cosmic body's plasmasphere where it extends away from the Sun, blown by the solar wind. Also known as *magnetotail,* somewhat inaccurately, since it is also possessed by planets that don't generate their own magnetic field, not to mention comets.

plasmoid
> A toroidal or round plasma structure that remains coherent over a substantial period of time; ball lightning, for example. Plasmoids are found in the planetary magnetospheres and are likely to exist at the centers of galaxies (in lieu of hypothetical black holes). Plasmoids are unstable, decaying into plasma jets.

P

polariton
> A quasi-particle representing the coupling of a photon with an excited quantum state. The states in question are called *plasmon, exciton,* or *phonon,* depending on the frequency of photons they can couple with. Polaritons are used in photonics to capture and guide light.
>
> See also *photonic network, polaritonic cloak,* and *waveguide.*

polaritonic cloak
> A surface of metamaterial that can capture light and guide it (as polaritons) around the protected body to release the photons at the opposite side, thus turning it invisible. Note, however, that the invisibility effect cannot be achieved on all frequencies at the same time, nor from all directions.
>
> Although it is usually referred to in popular science as *plasmonic cloak,* the excited quantum states that can couple with the photons (see the entry on *polariton,* above) needn't necessarily be plasmons. Because the common term in all cases is *polariton,* the choice was made to call this device a *polaritonic cloak* in *Pink Noise.*
>
> See also *metamaterial* and *polariton.*

pontine reticular formation
> A part of the brain involved in regulating the sleep/awake cycle.

power needle
> A kind of power generator in *Pink Noise* that draws power from the solar wind and also from dust devils drawn to it by the attractive force between parallel electric currents. Although extremely tall (but not as tall as a "space elevator"), they don't have to be built on the equator, because their stability is strengthened by this force.
>
> See also *dust devil, flywheel,* and *solar wind.*

prana [Sanskrit: पराण]
> Literally, "breath." In Hinduism, *prana* is the vital energy, permeating the cosmos and sustaining all living beings.

prayer flags
> In the Tibetan Buddhist worship, these are colorful pieces of fabric often found hanging on lines stretched along mountain trails.

LEONID KOROGODSKI

prayer wheels
An element of Tibetan Buddhist worship. Spinning a prayer wheel is considered the equivalent of uttering a prayer.

pyramidal tract
A neuronal pathway that connects the neocortex and the spinal cord. Also known as the *corticospinal tract.*

qhuqhumbela [Zulu]
A rhythmic, energetic Zulu dance with drums and handclaps as accompaniment.

raudram [Sanskrit: रौद्र]
The *rasa* of fury in Indian art and aesthetics. A *rasa* is the emotional response evoked in the audience by the artist.

relativistic time dilation
The phenomenon of time passing differently to different observers in special relativity. The faster one moves relative to another, the slower is the passage of time to the former. At the speed of light in vacuum, time stops.

Rényi entropies
A family of physical quantities that generalize the concept of entropy, a measure of disorder in a system.

revenant
In folklore, an undead returning from the grave to seek revenge.

right-hand rule
If the palm is the plane of the magnetic sail, oriented such that the magnetic field generated by the electric current in the sail points into the palm; and the four fingers show the direction of the solar wind; then the thumb, extending to the side, shows the thrust.

This is an equivalent rephrasing of the common mnemonic for determining the direction of the Lorentz force.

See also *magnetic sail.*

San
The Khoi and the San are the olive-skinned aborigenes of South Africa that have been living there since before the arrival of the Bantu tribes. While the Khoi were herders, the San were hunters and gatherers. Khoisan languages are rich in click consonants. They are the source of clicks in the Bantu languages in South Africa (for example, Xhosa and Zulu).

Also known as the Hottentots and the Bushmen, respectively, the Khoi and the San were categorized as the Colored racial category during the apartheid in South Africa.

single-threaded
When multiple tasks cannot be run in parallel.

singularity
A sudden, dramatic change in the state of a system, led there by incremental small changes.

sleepwalking
The phenomenon when a person walks, uses tools, and sometimes performs very complex actions—while asleep. Sleepwalking is *not* a conscious state like dreaming. It occurs during the deep stage of sleep.

solenoid
A kind of electromagnet, a solenoid is a spiral coil of wire that creates a magnetic field when conducting electric current.

solar storm
Powerful plasma eruptions from the Sun, much stronger than the normal solar wind. The speed of protons is known to reach at least the quarter of the speed of light on some occasions.

solar wind
A nearly continuous current of charged particles (net positive) that permeates the solar system, accelerated by the electric field of the Sun. One could say that we live within a tenuous extension of a star.

stack
In computer science, stack is a data structure that contains the information about the current state of an executing thread.

stem cell
An "unspecialized" cell that can potentially turn into any kind of cell in the body, from skin cells to neurons. Indeed, some research has already been done on turning skin cells into stem cells into neurons.

subcutaneous
Under the skin, like in "subcutaneous injection."

sublimation
The process of changing the state of matter from solid straight into gaseous, bypassing a liquid state.
See also *triple point.*

sulcus, *pl.* **sulci**
The distinctive furrows on the surface of the brain.

superconductivity
The phenomenon of zero electrical resistance in some materials at very low temperatures. A current in a superconductor can theoretically be maintained forever, since it loses no energy to resistance.

LEONID KOROGODSKI

Besides a rise in temperature beyond the critical value, superconductivity can be broken by the rise in electric current beyond a certain threshold, called the *critical current,* and similarly by the rise in magnetic field beyond the critical value.

superlens
A magnification device made of left-handed metamaterial. Since it doesn't have to be curved, a superlens can beat the diffraction limit on magnification, providing a view of objects smaller than the light's wavelength.
See also *metamaterial.*

swiss-cheese terrain
A unique terrain found at the Martian south polar cap, this is an often beautiful mosaic of shallow pits in the ice.
See also *Cryptic Region.*

synapse
A junction between neurons.

synchrotron radiation
Electromagnetic radiation with a characteristic signature, emitted by relativistic electrons accelerating across the field lines of a magnetic field. This is the most common kind of non-thermal radiation in space.

thalamus
Strategically placed at the center of the brain, the thalamus coordinates the process known as the *self.*

theta oscillations
Brain oscillations in the 4–8 hertz range produced in the hippocampus, theta oscillations are key players in memory formation and recall, navigation, and other hippocampal functions.

Tirukkural [Tᴀᴍɪʟ: திருக்குறள்]
A much celebrated classic of the ancient Tamil literature, *Tirukkural* is a collection of 1,330 rhyming aphorisms (*kurals*), composed by Tiruvalluvar circa the 2nd century BC. This is the first work on ethics in Indian literature.

Although less known in the West, the ancient Tamil literature is contemporary with the Vedas and rivals them in stature.

topgallant
A kind of sail.

topology
A field of mathematics studying the spatial properties that do not change during continuous transformations like stretching (tearing and gluing are not allowed).

T

triple point

The values of temperature and pressure at which the solid, liquid, and gaseous phases coexist. Below this point, liquid state is impossible and solids change straight into gas by the process called *sublimation*.

twasa [Zulu]

The ceremony in which a novice is accepted as an *isangoma*.

umkhovu, *pl.* **imikhovu** [Zulu]

A zombie, in the traditional Zulu worldview. To make one, *abathakathi* must dig a recent corpse out of the grave, pierce it with a stake, slit its tongue, and use certain medicines on it. After this, the deceased cannot become an ancestor shade, *idlozi*. This explains the old grave-watching custom, until the deceased comes to someone in a dream. Then it is understood that the ancestor has become a shade, the danger is past. But even so, king's widows were known to have watched their departed husband's grave for years.

See also *idlozi*.

King Dinuzulu's grave was still watched in 1966 by his last living widow [6]. The king died in 1913.

umthakathi, *pl.* **abathakathi** [Zulu]

An evil witch or sorcerer. In the traditional Zulu worldview, any untimely death or great disaster must be caused by a human agent. This is whence the concept of an *umthakathi* comes.

The traditional ways to kill an *umthakathi* are burning and impaling.

See also *isangoma* and *umkhovu*.

Unniyarcha [Malayalam: ഉണ്ണിയാർച്ച]

A legendary warrior woman celebrated in *Vadakkan Pattukal,* the Northern Ballads of Kerala. Unniyarcha belonged to the Chekavar caste and was skilled in *kalarippayatt,* especially with *urumi*.

See also *Chekavar, kalarippayatt,* and *urumi*.

urumi [Malayalam: ഉരുമി]

A weapon unique to the South Indian martial art of *kalarippayatt, urumi* is a flexible sword that can be worn inside a belt.

See also *kalarippayatt*.

waveguide

A structure that guides electromagnetic (that is, light) or sound waves.

See also *photonic network*.

Zulu Zionists

A brand of African Christianity, Zulu Zionism emphasizes prophetic dreams, faith healing, and allows polygamy. In some ways, the ministers are similar to *izangoma*. Zionism is also popular among the Swazi.

See also *African Christianity*.

Leonid Korogodski

PRONUNCIATION GUIDE

			ZULU				
CLICKS	c	Dental	Tongue against the upper teeth. Like the English *tsk* or *tut*.	ch	gc	nc	ngc
	q	Alveolar	Tongue against the palate. Like a bottle popping open.	qh	gq	nq	ngq
	x	Lateral	Made with the sides of the tongue (or with just one side).	xh	gx	nx	ngx
	Variants	Aspirated	Made with an audible puff of breath.	✕			
		Voiced	Like *g* with a simultaneous click.		✕		
		Nasal	Like *n* with a simultaneous click.			✕	
		Nasal	Like *ng* with a simultaneous click.				✕
OTHER CONSONANTS	h	Voiceless	Voiceless exhalation, as in *hat*. But *hh* is fully voiced, as in *aha!*	hh	Voiced		
	hl	Voiceless	With the tongue placed to say *l*, say *sh* — or *g* as in *genre*, for *dl*.	dl	Voiced		
	sh	Fricative	Like the English *sh*. But *tsh* is like the English *ch*.	tsh	Affricate		
	t	Unaspirated	As in *step*. But *th* is the aspirated *t*, with an audible puff, as in *top*.	th	Aspirated		
	p	Unaspirated	As in *pest*. But *ph* is the aspirated *p*, with an audible puff, as in *pot*.	ph	Aspirated		
	b	Implosive	No air leaves the mouth. But *bh* is like *b* in English, fully voiced.	bh	Aspirated		
	k	Unaspirated	As in *kill*, but is implosive in *uku-*. *Kh* is aspirated, as in *cat*.	kh	Aspirated		
	f	Voiceless	Both *f* and *v* are as in English.	v	Voiced		
	s	Voiceless	Both *s* and *z* are as in English.	z	Voiced		
	n	Alveolar	Both *n* and *ng* are as in English, except *ny* is as *gn* in *vignette*.	ng	Palatal		
	m	Labial	As in English.				
	l	Approximant	As in Spanish. Softer than in English.				
	y	Approximant	As in English.				
	w	Approximant	As in English.				
	d	Voiced	As in English.				
	j	Voiced	As in English.				
	g	Voiced	As in *go*, but fully voiced. Never as in *gin* or *genre*.				
VOWELS	a		Always as in *mama*. Never as in *ma'am*.				
	i		Always as *ee* in *seek*. Never as in *sit* nor *site*.				
	u		Always as *oo* in *book*. Never as in *dud* nor *dude*.				
	e	Open	As in *bed*, in most cases. Closed in final syllables or before a syllable with an *i* or a *u*, sounding as *a* in *bay* but without the *y*.	e	Closed		
	o	Open	As in *bog*, in most cases. Closed in final syllables or before a syllable with an *i* or a *u*, sounding as in *bow* but without the *w*.	o	Closed		

Hl is like the Welsh *ll*.

Don't confuse *th* and *ph* with the English ones!

Kl is sometimes pronounced like a sharp guttural click. But this rare sound has almost disappeared already.

Like all South African languages, with the exception of English and Afrikaans, the Zulu language has clicks and aspirated consonants, pronounced with a puff of breath.

But if you think that Zulu has a difficult pronunciation, wait until you're introduced to Irish, Tamil, Malayalam, Sanskrit, and Mandarin Chinese.

Although Irish sounds may be (relatively) less exotic, the spelling rules require many pages to describe. Malayalam spelling is consistent, but its sounds are even more exotic than in Zulu! And all four Asian languages used here have *different* non-Latin scripts.

Since only a handful of words appear in the story from the Asian languages, only their approximate pronunciation is given, using the closest English sounds, without going into more detail. The stressed syllables are capitalized, unless there is only one.

OTHER LANGUAGES			
CHINESE	Xīng	星	This word means *star* in Mandarin Chinese. The *x* stands for a sound between *sh* and *s,* pronounced with the tongue lying flat, touching the lower teeth. The word is pronounced in the high flat tone.
IRISH	bean sidhe		Approximation in English: *byan shee*. The *b* is a "slender" consonant, which is to the "broad" *b* (as in English) what the *gn* in *vignette* is to *n* in *not*.
IRISH	Lough-an-Leagh		Approximation in English: *Lohh-ahn-Lyahh,* where *hh* is a voiced exhalation (like in Zulu, see above). The first *L* is "broad," and the second one is "slender," like *gl* in Italian.
MALAYALAM	ankam	അങ്കം	Approximation in English: *AHN-kahm*.
MALAYALAM	Chekavar	ചേകവർ	Approximation in English: *Che-kah-VAR*.
MALAYALAM	meyya kannakuka	മെയ്യ കണ്ണാക്കുക	Approximation in English: *MEH-yyah KAH-nnah-guh*.
MALAYALAM	Unniyarcha	ഉണ്ണിയാർ ച്ച	Approximation in English: *Oo-nnee-YAR-chah*.
MALAYALAM	urumi	ഉരുമി	Approximation in English: *oo-ROO-mee*.
TAMIL SAN.	raudram	रौद्रं	Approximation in English: *rah-OO-drahm*. Note that *au* is not a diphtong.
TAMIL SAN.	Tirukkural	திருக்குறள்	Essentially, a concatenation of two words. Approximation in English: *Tee-ROOK Koo-RAHL*.

LEONID KOROGODSKI

ACKNOWLEDGEMENTS

THIS STORY BEGAN AT THE 10TH ANNIVERSARY REUNION OF the Viable Paradise writers workshop on Martha's Vineyard in 2006, as a homework exercise on a suggested theme: *Fairies and Flamethrowers.*

I wish to express my heartfelt gratitude to the VP9 instructors—Patrick and Teresa Nielsen Hayden, editors at Tor®; and the authors Debra Doyle, Steven Gould, Jim Macdonald, and Laura Mixon—as well as the other students and staff, for helping me hone my writing skills, and everyone who commented on the story in its earliest incarnation at the reunion. A special thank you goes to Suzanne Palmer, a VP9 graduate, for organizing the reunion and suggesting the theme.

Before I attended Viable Paradise, I had learned much about writing from Kij Johnson at the Center for the Study of Science Fiction Novel Writing Workshop and from Marta Randall at Gotham Writing Workshops. While working on *Pink Noise,* I received helpful comments from many people, at the Science Fiction and Fantasy Online Writing Workshop (sff.onlinewritingworkshop.com), Authonomy, Baen's Bar, and in the face-to-face critique groups of which I was or am a member: Boston Critters, Second Supper, and Newport Round Table, the latter organized by Mark Ellis and Melissa Martin Ellis.

A modified excerpt from the first chapter of *Pink Noise* won first prize in the contest for the best prose poem under 500 words in speculative fiction at Odyssey Con 2009, judged by Joe Haldeman, and was published in the convention's proceedings under the title, *100 seconds from the Century of Martian Wars*. I would like to thank the organizer of the contest, a poet and VP graduate, F.J. Bergmann.

When researching the scientific aspects of the story, I was privileged to have many stimulating conversations with Rodolfo Llinás of New York University School of Medicine (who, among other things, suggested the clockface metaphor in Chapter 3) and Anthony Peratt of Los Alamos National Laboratory. I have also learned from Eric Lerner and members of the Thunderbolts group (thunderbolts.info): Donald Scott, Wallace Thornhill, David Talbott, and many others.

The publication of this book was made possible by the generous support of Elizabeth Bell Carroll, Mikhail Faktorovich, and my brother, Alexander Korogodsky.

As the book's editor, Elizabeth rescued me from making some embarrassing mistakes and pushed me into finding better turns of phrase in certain places where I would have otherwise remained content with what I had. Guddah of guddah.com took the story to heart and made the illustrations for the story and the cover art. He also did an awesome job on my website, pinknoise.net. I am truly fortunate to have such good friends.

Simon A. Forward helped to write the pitch, found on the front flap of the dust jacket. Many thanks to Jane Frank of wow-art.com for teaching me the importance of illustrations and the much needed harangue on all the things that possibly can go wrong. To Frank Nemeyer of SCORE for his advice, emphasizing the importance of distribution. To Jennifer Grahovac, Rod Kneiper, and Mike Topovsky of BookMasters® Inc., this book's distributor and fulfilment company, for seeing me through this part of the business. I am indebted to Alan Litovsky for his legal help, and to Jeff Danziger for his invaluable support.

LEONID KOROGODSKI

Nqina Dlamini, Sibusiso Mbokazi, and other members of the isizulu.net community translated for me some of the Zulu phrases. Jessy and Manoj Varghese helped me with the Malayalam. Any mistakes that may remain are mine.

Many thanks to Falit Pandya, a director of Print Vision Pvt. Ltd., for his help in literally putting *Pink Noise* on paper and considerable patience in answering my questions. I am also grateful to Marcia Santos of Kirkwood Printing, who oversaw printing of the 50 Advance Reading Copies, as well as everyone at Acme Bookbinding that printed and bound them.

Special thank you to the writers who gave their time to reading this book and commenting on it.

The people who helped me at various stages of the project are many. I apologize in advance if the following list is incomplete. Thanks go to Jason Ahlquist, Kweku Asumang, Lucia Bibolini, Jak Brienhead, Sara "Azbukivedi" Bukin, Maria Bustillos, Kurt Campbell, Karen Carr, S. Harrison Carter Jr., John Chu, Carlos Jiménez-Cortés, Susan Curnow, Rob Davies, Bea Deen, Linda DiPalma, Nancy L. Driggs, Mark Ellis, Melissa Martin Ellis, Robert Gardner, Stephen Gallup, Peter Greenwell, Jessica Grota, Whitley Hodges, L. David Holbrook Jr., Corin Sän Inman, Patty Jansen, Zak Jarvis, Brenda Kalt, Dave King, Katherine J. Koss Smith, Adrian Krag, Susan Kurz, Betsey LaMonte, Laura Lascarso, Nicole J. LeBoeuf-Little, Greg London, Karin Lowachee, Eric Lowe, Amy Machado, Edith Maor, Helen Mazarakis, John McCallum, Lucille McDonald, Kathleen McKenzie, Laura Mixon, Sharon Mock, Ian Morrison, Dave Newbury, Paul Newlands, Gil Paradis, Jennifer Pelland, Michael Pomerantsev, Jonathan J. Prescott-Roy, Wayne Quackenbush, Ruthanne Reid, Anthony Saunders, Jacqueline Schumann, Richard Scott, Jeremy Shattuck, Thomas J. Sherlock, S. Chris Shirley, Thomas E. Smith, Tracey Ann Stewart, Jesse Tate, Douglas Texter, Michael Torrington, Ian Tregillis, Doreen Tucker, Corinna Turner, Petronella Vrolyk, Geoff Whyte, Walter Williams, and Billy Young.

Last but not least, I want to thank my family and friends for their support and understanding.

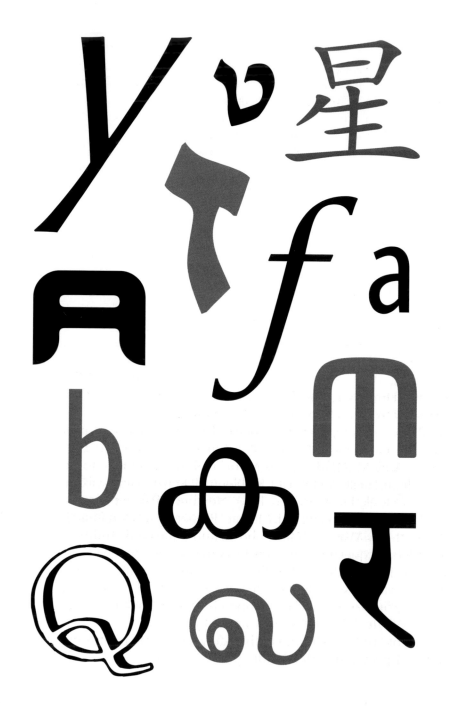

COLOPHON

THE PRIMARY TYPEFACE IN *PINK NOISE* IS OPTIMA NOVA®. Designed in the 1950s by Hermann Zapf (b. 1918), one of the most celebrated font designers of the 20th century, the original Optima® has a distinguished history. It is a humanist sans serif font with such fine curves and tapers that they effectively play the part of serifs. This kind of subtle variation is what the brain likes to see, making the font easy to read. But because of these delicate tapers, this font has been a challenge to convert into a digital format. The first attempt, also called Optima, had to sacrifice too much because of the stair-stepping effect at the low resolution of the monitor's screen.

Optima nova (Copyright © 2003 Linotype® GmbH) is the second, more successful attempt by Akira Kobayashi and Hermann Zapf, to create a digital version of Optima. It also has a true italic (not merely slanted) and a titling face.

What other font shows so well the loss one suffers in the conversion to a digital format?

The other fonts used in *Pink Noise*:

- Agilita® Condensed, by Jürgen Weltin. A "sans serif companion" to Optima nova. Copyright © 2006 Linotype® GmbH.
- Neo® Tech, by Sebastian Lester, designed to look futuristic but not gimmicky. Copyright © 2004 Monotype® Imaging, Inc.

- **AURA**, a titling typeface by Jackson Burke. Copyright © 1998 T.26. Appears on the dust jacket and the spine of the cover.
- MONUMENT, another distinguished titling face, by Oldřich Menhart (1897–1962). Digitized by Dieter Steffman. Copyright © 2002 Typographer Mediengestaltung. Appears in the Latin quote of the Occam's Razor principle on page 176.
- Narkis Classic Hebrew, by Zvi Narkis (b. 1921). Appears on page 61 in the Biblical allusion expanded on the facing page. Copyright © 2003 MasterFont®.
- Rachana, by K.H. Hussein, is a free Malayalam typeface that reintroduced hundreds of beautiful *akhand* glyphs, which had been removed from the language in the pre-computer age to map the alphabet onto the typewriter's keyboard. Having ushered in the Malayalam typographic renaissance, Rachana is now a component of the Linux-based Rachana operating system. Copyright © 2005 Rachana Akshara Vedi.
- Thunaivan TSC, a free Tamil font by Ravindran Paul. Copyright © 2002 Micro Mart. Appears in the epigraphical inscription and appendices.
- Sanskrit 2003. Copyright © 2004 Omkarananda Ashram Himalayas. Used in appendices.
- Adobe® Kaiti, a Chinese and Japanese font. Copyright © 2006 Adobe Systems Inc. Used in appendices.

THIS BOOK IS PRINTED BY PRINT VISION PVT. LTD. IN Ahmedabad, India, a winner of several National and South Asian awards of Excellence in Printing.

The text is printed on BILT Sinnar Silk 80# with black and magenta inks. The internal illustrations are in "four-color black," with a spot UV glossy coating. The dust jacket is printed on BILT Sinnar Glossy 100# with the four-color CMYK process (Cyan, Magenta, Yellow, and blacK), as well as Pantone® Goe® 31-1-3, a pearlescent overprint varnish, and an application of the "strike-through" technique: a spot UV matte coating, followed up by a flood UV glossy coating, such that the latter is neutralized over the matte areas.

LEONID KOROGODSKI

ויעש יי אלהים לאדם

ולאשתו כתנות עור וילבשם

3:21 בראשית—

And made **** ELOHIM for Adam

and for his wife garments of skin,

and clothed them.

—GENESIS, 3:21

Layered Terrain, West Arabia Terra Crater, Mars.
Credits: NASA / JPL / Malin Space Science Systems.